Death Dealers Incorporated

By Robert Fisher

Death Dealers Incorporated
Copyright © 2020 Robert Fisher
ISBN: 978-1-970153-25-5

The main protagonists in this novel are fiction. Any similarity to persons living or dead is coincidental. Of the actual historical individuals mentioned, every effort had been made to keep their words, intentions and actions consistent with recorded history. The endeavor was to follow chronological events as they relate to the narrative.

La Maison Publishing, Inc.
Vero Beach, Florida
The Hibiscus City
lamaisonpublishing@gmail.com

Contents

Chapter 1

Death Wears Hawaiian Shirts

Mack Roycewicz reclined on the bed of his hotel room while reading the latest issue of Justice League. He brought it with him to Stockholm to read while waiting for his target to show up. Occasionally he would glance out the window to see if the target had arrived. On the floor next to the bed lay a large guitar case. Across the street from the hotel was the home of his target a man named Lars Kinski, a high ranking member of a Swedish pro fascist militant group.

Mack was wearing his red Hawaiian shirt with a green leaf pattern, khaki pants and a black t-shirt under his Hawaiian shirt. Mack checked his watch. It read 9:00 pm which meant Kinski was due to arrive any minute. As he returned to the comic book, his mind flashed back to several weeks ago when he accepted this job from the Guild. The contract on Kinski was open and put out by an Israeli millionaire whose daughter was killed by Kinski's militant group while touring Europe. He had been covertly tracking Kinski for a week learning his habits and routines.

Suddenly the faint sound of a car pulling up outside caught his attention, he checked his watch, it read 9:30.

"Bastards late for his own funeral" muttered Roycewicz as he quickly got off the bed. He pulled a pair of black gloves out of his pocket and put them on.

He opened the guitar case and pulled out a McMillan Alias CS5 sniper rifle with a scope and silencer. Casually he placed a fresh clip into the rifle casually and approached the window.

Mack disliked using sniper rifles but he soon realized his methods were not suitable for this job so he ordered the rifle from the Guild. He aimed the rifle out the window making sure to keep that barrel from sticking out. Mack smiled, recognizing the car as the one driven by Kinski's chauffer. Gingerly Mack opened the window a few inches so he could fire without damaging the window. Mack raised the rifle's scope to his eye, taking care not to have the barrel point out the window.

Kinski got out of the car and spoke to the driver before closing the door. Once the car was gone, Kinski began walking up the steps to the front door. Mack lined up the crosshairs on the back of Kinski's head, took a deep breath to steady the rifle, and pulled the trigger. Instantly Kinski fell to the ground dead as bits of his blood, bone and brain lay strewn across the yard. Mack put the rifle back in the guitar case then closed the window.

Usually Mack took no pleasure in killing but he had to admit it felt good to take revenge on a man who believed his people had no right to live. He took the gloves off and returned them to his pocket. Mack pulled his cellphone out of his pocket and sent a text that read: Kinski contract completed by MAGIC 44, to a number that read GUILD. He put the phone back in his pocket then pulled his suitcase out from under the bed and placed it on the bed. Ever since he arrived in Sweden he couldn't help but feel he had forgotten something. When he finished packing his suitcase his phone suddenly began to ring.

He pulled it out to see what it said, even though he had a good idea what the message was. It was a text response from the Guild stating that the money for killing Kinski had been placed in his account and that they would send a cleaner to retrieve the rifle and remove all traces of his presence there. Mack smiled in satisfaction at getting the nine hundred thousand dollars as he put the phone in his pocket. He looked around the room to make sure he didn't forget anything. After triple checking, he walked out the door but he still couldn't help but feel like he had forgotten something.

He returned his room key to the front desk and exited the building. He walked to his rented car in the parking lot next to the hotel and placed his suitcase in the back seat. He opened the driver side front door, got in and started the car. He was glad to finally be going home to his penthouse in New York. Suddenly he snapped his fingers realizing what it was that he had forgotten.

"Dammit, I forgot to DVR the Walking Dead" muttered Mack angrily.

He shrugged his shoulders dismissively and drove to the airport confident that he would be able to catch up via reruns and marathons.

Chapter 2

Same Old Same Old

Dennis Faraday sat at his cubicle desk at Minute Broadcasting headquarters in New York City. He stared blankly at his computer screen like a zombie. His head being held up by his left hand as he slowly began to fall asleep. He was an average man of medium build with short black hair and glasses. He was wearing a white dress shirt with a black tie and grey pants.

The office around him was a seemingly endless row of cubicles with the sounds of typing and talking filling the air drenched in fluorescent light. His co-workers would joke that the fluorescent lights sucked the life out of everyone, right now it felt less like a joke and more like a fact as his eyelids grew heavier. As he sat at the desk sleeping his head began to slide slowly out of his hand. His head fell out of his hand and hit the desk waking him up abruptly.

"Damn" muttered Faraday now wide-awake, he straightened his black tie and adjusted his glasses.

He yawned and decided to go to the break room and get some coffee. He picked up his coffee mug and walked to the break room. Upon arriving at the break room he saw two men seated at a table watching CNN on a TV in the corner of the ceiling. Ignoring them, he walked to the coffee maker on the counter and was pleased to see that there was still some coffee left in the pot. He poured some coffee into his mug followed by two sugars and some half-and-half.

After stirring it with a small disposable plastic spoon he took a large gulp of coffee. Feeling recharged, he shifted his attention to the TV. He walked over to the two men watching TV and stood behind them.

"What's going on guys?" asked Faraday before taking another sip of coffee.

"Some politician got shot in Sweden" answered one of the men.

"Who was he?" Faraday asked.

"Lars Kinski" answered one of the men gesturing to the TV.

"Who?" asked Faraday. "Some neo Nazi leader" answered the other man at the table.

"Huh" said Faraday finding it hard to have any kind of sympathy for a dead neo Nazi.

"They find who did it?" asked Faraday.

"No, not a trace" replied the other man. A few minutes later the story changed and Faraday returned to his cubicle having lost interest in the news.

He sat down at his desk, and glanced at the digital clock next to his computer it read 4:00 pm. Is this what it's come to he asked himself as he couldn't help but reflect on his status in life. After graduating High School in his native Baltimore he got a scholarship to New York University and decided to pursue his dream being a writer. While he was at NYU he spent all his free time writing a book while learning how to. After graduating he managed to get the book published.

Unfortunately the sales were low and the reviews poor. Desperate for cash, having spent almost all his money trying to get published, he considered his options aside from having a bachelor's degree in English and literature he had a degree in computer engineering and accounting. So he applied for, and got, a job at the headquarters of Minute Broadcasting as a computer programmer in New York City where he's worked for the last three years. He sighed irritated at how boring his life was compared to what he thought it would be like when he was in High School back in Baltimore. Instead of living in a mansion in Miami he was living in an apartment in Brooklyn that he could barely afford.

Instead of being married to a supermodel he had just been dumped by his girlfriend. He shrugged his shoulders, and straightened his glasses and returned to work. As he resumed his daily drudgery he prayed that something somehow would happen that would upset the monotony of his life.

Chapter 3

24.497226, 139.327318

Scattered all over the world, are places where the depraved, the dangerous and the desperate can go and live outside of the laws of men. One such place is the island of Sankan, located in the region of the Philippine Sea dubbed the Devils Sea. The islands ownership has been in limbo since the Second World War. On the northern half of the island are mountains, forests and a volcano surrounded by boiling pits of sulfuric acid.

On the southern half of the island is a small city unimaginatively called Sankan City.

Though the city and the island enjoys a far more unique nickname mentioned only in hushed whispers: The capital city of crime or more appropriately hell. The city is divided and ruled over by two of the world's largest criminal organizations: The Heise She li triad from Hong Kong and the Vasilev Syndicate from Moscow who have coexisted peacefully for twenty years. The skyline of the city is dominated by two skyscrapers each one belonging to the triad and the syndicate. The mammoth structures serve as the regional headquarters for their respective organizations and as the domiciles of the individual assigned to control the island by their leaders.

In the triads building, one of those individuals, a Chinese man named Deng sat at his desk in his office. Six months ago the Mountain Master made a deal with a former CIA agent, named Simon Kane, to rescue the

Mountain Master's daughter, Mai Yunao, from the Rojas Cartel. In exchange the triad would aid him in destroying their mutual enemy, the enigmatic criminal organization known as the Networc, by assembling a team to help him find the Networc within the next six months. While the triad was tracking down the team, Simon would be acting as Mai's bodyguard. The Mountain Master had tasked Deng with finding the members of the team.

After searching for three months they found and recruited one member, a former IRA assassin turned catholic nun named Siobhan Costello. Unfortunately after two months of searching they had yet to locate the third member of the team: the freelance assassin codenamed MAGIC 44. Suddenly, Deng's assistant burst into the room brandishing a folder and an excited grin, interrupting Deng's recollection.

"Let me guess: you've got good news" said Deng as he leaned back in his chair.

"The best Sir, we've found him" said Mazin as he sat in one of the chairs in front of the desk.

"You're kidding" said Deng as he tossed the folder on the desk.

"Where is he?" asked Deng.

"En route to New York from Stockholm" Mazin answered.

"Must have been doing a contract, how'd you find out?" asked Deng as he picked up the folder and began skimming through it.

"I contacted a friend of mine at the Guild, apparently he's been busy lately" answered Mazin.

"Impressive, the Guild doesn't usually reveal the locations of their clients" said Deng as he continued skimming through the folder.

"True, but here's the funny thing, that's only when they're on a contract and he just finished one in Stockholm" replied Mazin. For the next few seconds they were quiet as Deng continued reading. Once he finished reading the papers in the folder he closed it and placed the folder back on his desk.

"So, what's the plan, want me to contact our New York branch and have them recruit him" asked Mazin.

"No, I want to handle this myself" Deng answered.

"Sir if I may ask, why?" asked Mazin confused and surprised.

"I want to see what Siobhan can do in the field" answered Deng.

Mazin's confusion only grew upon hearing Deng's answer. Ever since Siobhan arrived on Sankan two months ago, she had been working day and night at the various soup kitchens operated by the triad.

"What does she have to do with this?" asked Mazin.

"It's simple, she has the reputation of being one of the most dangerous people on the planet, yet in the two months she's been here she's done nothing to prove it" said Deng.

"Hell, you threaten her she just says God bless you or some shit, so what better way to see if her reputation is earned than by having her be my bodyguard while I'm in New York in case the Networc or the Scarpetta family try anything" continued Deng.

Mazin understood Deng's reasoning for involving Siobhan, though he didn't agree with it. However he had to admit it made perfect sense considering the triad's New York branch had a history of problems with the La Cosa Nostra of New York.

"Doesn't this violate that deal you made with her in exchange for her help" asked Mazin.

"No, that deal expires once we've crippled the Networc" answered Deng.

"Speaking of which, where is Siobhan right now?" Deng asked curiously.

Mazin pulled out his phone to check, "She's at the kitchen downtown" replied Mazin.

"I gotta stop asking stupid questions" Deng said with a shrug.

"Good advice" replied Deng sarcastically.

"Do you want me to tell her to come back?" replied Mazin.

Deng thought for a minute, "Have her brought her here, I'll brief her myself might as well, I want to be in New York asap" answered Deng.

"Incidentally I believe Simon and Mai are working in Peru right now right?" asked Deng.

"Yeah Lima, why?" Mazin replied.

"I think it's time to check up on them, besides we have to refuel there anyway" answered Deng.

Mazin shrugged, "I'll notify the airport at once and have your plane prepared to go".

"As soon as possible" continued Deng, "Understood" said Mazin as he stood up to leave. Around an hour or so later, Siobhan walked into Deng's office. She was wearing her black and white nun's habit and her gold necklace with a cross on it around her neck.

Casually she walked to the chair in front of Deng's desk and sat down.

"You wanted to see me?" said Siobhan in her lyrical Irish accent as polite as usual.

Deng leaned back in his chair.

"Yes I did, remember how I said you were going to be a member of a team we were putting together?" asked Deng.

"Well, we found the final member of the team, he's an assassin based out of New York and I'm going to go recruit him" continued Deng.

"However we have a rather…tenuous with the New York branch of the Scarpetta family" said Deng.

"So you want me to go with you as your bodyguard while you're there" Siobhan replied flatly.

Deng snapped his fingers, "couldn't have said it better myself" said Deng with a grin.

"However, we'll be making a stopover in Peru first" said Deng.

Siobhan raised an eyebrow suspiciously, "why?"

"To introduce you to the leader of the team, his names Simon Kane" answered Deng as he handed Siobhan a picture of Simon. She studied the picture: he was a clean shaven, muscular man with slicked back, short black hair, and a black eye patch over his right eye. He was dressed in black buttoned shirt with the top two buttons undone, dark green pants and a long dark blue trench coat.

"In case you're wondering about his qualifications he was a Navy SEAL before being inducted into some black ops division of the CIA, any questions?" explained Deng as she continued studying the picture.

"What about this girl he is protecting?" asked Siobhan.

"She's none of your business, any other questions?" said Deng bluntly.

"This organization you mentioned you called them the Networc yes?" asked Siobhan. "That's right" replied Deng.

"Why does he want to destroy them?" asked Siobhan.

Deng took off his sunglasses and sighed before putting them back on. "We don't know the details but eight months ago an agent of theirs killed his wife" answered Deng.

"Do you believe he can be trusted?" asked Siobhan.

"Yes, do you?" asked Deng.

"I've worked with people motivated by the death of a loved one it never ends well" answered Siobhan.

"I can see why you'd say that but the Mountain Master trusted him to rescue and bodyguard his daughter so he's not crazy" said Deng.

"You can put your trust in the Mountain Master, I'll put mine in the lord" said Siobhan.

Chapter 4

Two guys walk into a bar....

Typically Dennis was not the last person to leave the office. Tonight however, because of a mountain of paperwork that his boss dropped on him, he was leaving much later than usual. He walked out the front door of the Minute broadcasting building and glanced up at the building contemptuously. He shifted his attention to his watch; it read 9:30 pm, then to the street.

"Dammit" muttered Dennis once again lamenting the loss of his car which for the last week had been under repair.

He straightened his glasses and looked around for any taxis. After about ten minutes one began to approach, frantically Dennis began waving his free hand to get its attention. Dennis breathed a sigh of relief when it stopped. He got inside the cab, told the driver his address and they began driving down the street. As they drove to Dennis's apartment he gazed out the window.

People and signs on the street were reduced to a formless hypnotic blur, the darkness of night held at bay by the twinkling lights of the city. Once they crossed the Brooklyn Bridge he began feeling thirsty. He looked for a bar or a convenience store where he could get a drink. Suddenly he spotted one and told the driver to pull over. Grudgingly the driver pulled up to the sidewalk.

Dennis handed the driver an extra twenty dollars to wait for him. He got out of the car and looked at the sign on the door, it read Carlito's pub. He shrugged and entered the bar. There were four men in the bar including the bartender. Two of them were passed out drunk in a booth, the other man was sitting at the bar watching TV occasionally taking a sip of a clear liquid Dennis just assumed was Vodka. The bartender, a large disgruntled looking man was behind the bar cleaning it with a rag.

Not being much of a drinker, Dennis approached the bar and ordered a glass of ginger ale. Upon hearing his order the bartender's face contorted in mild annoyance.

"3.50" groused the bartender as he began pouring the drink.

"Who the hell walks into a bar and orders soda?" complained the bartender as he handed Dennis the beverage.

"People that like soda" said the man at the other end of the bar with a sarcastic grin.

Dennis couldn't help but laugh at the remark. "Fucking smartass" muttered the bartender as he shifted his attention to the cash register.

As Dennis drank the ginger ale he noticed the man at the other end of the bar looking at him as if he was trying to figure out who he was. The man at the other end of the bar had short spiky blonde hair and was wearing a red unbuttoned Hawaiian shirt that had a pattern of green leaves on it with a black t-shirt underneath and khaki pants. He appeared to be Dennis's age and height but with a more muscular athletic frame. His frame reminded him of a kid that used to bully him in elementary school.

"Can I help you?" asked Dennis.

"You look familiar" answered the man at the other end of the bar.

"I do?" asked Dennis somewhat confused; suddenly the man snapped his fingers as if he just realized something.

"I got it, you wrote that book a few years ago what was it called" said the man as he tried to remember the title.

"Black Spear right?" the man asked excitedly.

Dennis didn't know what was more surprising the fact that he was meeting someone that read the book or that someone read it in the first place. "Yeah I wrote that" he answered.

The man clapped his hands in surprise. "Awesome, I loved that book man" said the man.

"Really?" said Dennis surprised.

"It's a crime that it didn't sell more copies" said the man as he walked towards him. He sat in a stool next to Dennis and turned to face him.

"Thanks" replied Dennis, "I'm surprised to meet someone that read it at all much less liked it" continued Dennis.

"Yeah man those critics couldn't be more wrong" said the man. "Speaking of which I can't remember your name, what is it? It's been a while since I read the book" he continued.

"Dennis Faraday, what's yours?" asked Dennis, "Mack, Mack Roycewicz" answered the man.

"That's an interesting name" replied Dennis before taking another sip of soda.

"Yeah, my mom was a huge Bobby Darin fan, you know Mack the knife" answered Mack.

"Huh" replied Dennis mildly surprised.

"It's probably none of my damn business but are you working on another book?" asked Mack.

"Well since the book failed to make any money my publisher dropped me and I got a job as a computer programmer at Minute Broadcasting a few years ago" answered Dennis.

"Man, what a waste of talent, hell in my opinion, it's just as good as the Action Hero Squad" replied Mack sympathetically.

"The Action Hero Squad?" asked Dennis questioningly.

"Yeah you know, it was written by Sheila Goodbody" said Mack sounding like a Star Wars fan that met someone who never heard of Star Wars.

"Who?" replied Dennis.

"Sheila Goodbody, she died in that car accident a few months ago?" continued Mack.

"Oh yeah, her" said Dennis half remembering. "So what do you do?" he asked.

Mack grinned slyly at the question, "Let's just say, I travel a lot" answered Mack.

"Interesting, where were you last?" asked Dennis enviously.

"Stockholm" answered Mack.

Dennis was somewhat annoyed at how he dodged the question when suddenly he remembered the waiting taxi outside. "Excuse me, I have to go I forgot that my taxi's waiting for me outside" said Dennis as he hurriedly placed some money on the counter. Frantically he ran outside only to see that the taxi was gone. He looked up and down the street for it but it was gone.

"Son of a bitch" he muttered as a few raindrops started to crash onto the pavement. Half a minute later, Mack walked out of the bar and was surprised to see Dennis standing there.

"What happened?" asked Mack incredulously.

"My taxi left me here, guess I'm walking home" muttered Dennis as he turned to leave.

"How about a lift?" said Mack.

Dennis turned around surprised at the offer, "What, no I couldn't" protested Dennis politely but feeling stupid for denying the help.

"Don't worry about it; it's no skin off my ass, hell I was going home anyway" replied Mack warmly.

"Alright" said Dennis.

"Great, my cars around back, follow me" said Mack.

Dennis followed Mack through an alley to the parking lot behind the bar. Mack's car was a red 1973 Ford XB Falcon GT Coupe.

"Hell of a car" said Dennis upon seeing it, for some reason it looked familiar but he couldn't figure out why.

"Thanks I restored it myself, cost a couple thousand to restore but it was so worth it" said Mack proudly.

"It looks familiar" said Dennis.

"It should; it's the same make and model as the one from the Road Warrior" answered Mack as he opened the front passenger door.

Dennis nodded and sat in the seat, Mack quickly walked to the other side of the car, opened the driver side door and sat behind the wheel. He turned the key and the car growled to life.

"Where do you live?" asked Mack, Dennis gave him his address and they drove out of the parking lot. As they drove down the street Dennis couldn't but wonder how Mack could afford to restore the car the way he did.

"I'm sorry to bring this back up but, what is your job again?" asked Dennis nervously. Mack looked at him with an imposing but sly look on his face.

"Do you really want to know?" asked Mack with a sly grin.

"Well with an answer like that I kinda have to know now" Dennis replied.

Mack laughed, "You got a point" he replied as he returned his gaze to the road in front of him.

"There are a lot of words for what I do but I guess the best possible word for what I do is freelance hitman" answered Mack.

"Come on" replied Dennis grinning, thinking he was joking.

"I'm serious" replied Mack drily.

"Okay prove it" said Dennis thinking he was being set up for a joke.

Mack thought for a minute trying to think of how to prove it when it occurred to him. "Alright, did you hear about that guy that was shot in Stockholm?" asked Mack.

Dennis searched his memory for what he meant when he suddenly remembered his conversation in the break room earlier today.

"Yeah," replied Dennis.

"That was me, shot him from a window across the street with a McMillan Alias CS5" continued Mack.

Dennis thought for a minute, the level of detail lent some veracity to what he said especially considering that the authorities hadn't revealed what kind of gun was used in the killing.

"It still seems a bit far-fetched" replied Dennis.

"Fine I've got an idea, I'm going up to Toronto to do a job this weekend come with me and write about it" said Mack.

"What?" replied Dennis in surprise.

"Seriously, you're a writer and once I've looked over it obviously you sell the story to the papers or make it into a book or some shit" said Mack as they pulled to a stop in front of Faraday's apartment.

"Tell you what; todays Monday and I'm leaving Friday afternoon for the job so that gives you two days to think about it" continued Mack. He pulled a piece of paper and a pen out of his pocket and scribbled some numbers on it.

"If you want in, call me at this number" said Mack as he handed the paper to Dennis.

Dennis nodded in understanding, "thanks for the lift" said Dennis as he got out of the car.

"Don't worry about it" replied Mack dismissively before driving away.

Dennis looked down at the piece of paper in his hand just as the ramifications of that conversation began to occur to him.

Chapter 5

Negotiable Assets

The airstrip was surrounded on all sides by the Chiles barren Atacama Desert. The lifeless plateau resembled that of another planet as it stretched on word for miles. Simon Kane had been waiting there for hours, asleep in the back of the car that brought him to the airstrip. For the last five months he had been traveling across the world acting as Mai's bodyguard, while she did her charity work, and frankly he was sick of it. Although, in the five months he'd been body guarding her he had come to look at Mai differently.

He theorized that it was because of what they went through five months ago on Sankan established some kind of bond between them. Occasionally Simon wondered if she had any affection for him, with the exception of Simon's black eye patch covering his right eye he was still attractive in a scruffy kind of way. His late wife, Sheila, once said he was handsome in an Indiana Jones kind of way but he brushed these thoughts aside. He knew they would only be friends and he was fine with it. After his wife was killed by the Networc eight months ago he vowed to never put someone he loved in danger.

His mind flashed back to the events of last night, while he was sleeping on the couch in there hotel room and while Mai was asleep in the bed. There was a knock on the door of their room. When he opened the door, there were three Chinese men from the Triad standing there. Two of them were there to watch Mai while the other one was going to drive him to the airstrip for what he had no idea. Simon quickly got dressed in his dark green pants, black short sleeve dress shirt then grabbed his dark blue trench coat, pistol wrist blade and followed the man to the car.

Once they were in the car the driver took his weapons and they drove off. Suddenly a loud familiar buzzing sound ended his reverie; he looked out the window of the car and saw a plane getting closer. Within minutes the plane came barreling down the runway until it finally stopped. Simon and the driver got out of the car. Once again he cursed himself for wearing the trench coat in the middle of the desert.

The driver stood by the car while Simon approached the plane somewhat sure of who was inside. As Simon approached the plane the door opened onto the pavement, it had stairs on the other side. Down the stairs walked Deng wearing his black suit and black tea shade sunglasses followed by Siobhan.

While Simon assumed Deng was onboard he did not expect to see the woman that followed Deng out of the plane. She was, despite the sweltering desert heat, wearing the black and white habit of a catholic nun and a gold necklace with a cross on it.

Simon dismissed her realizing that the reason why Deng brought a Catholic nun with him would be answered later. Simon and Deng walked up to each other and shook hands.

"Greetings Mr. Kane, it's been awhile" said Deng as they shook hands.

"Time flies when you're having fun" Simon replied sarcastically.

Deng grinned at the wisecrack while the woman's face remained impassive. "Before we continue any further, let's talk inside shall we?" he said gesturing to the plane.

"If you insist" said Simon drily as he followed them into the cooler confines of the plane.

The interior was comfortable and luxurious, against the left and right wall sat two expensive looking brown leather chairs with an equally expensive looking wooden coffee table between the two. Simon sat in the chair on the left while Deng sat in the chair on the right, the woman stood next to him, her arms folded like she was a bodyguard. Simon sighed in relief at being out of the hot desert sun.

"So, what's this all about Deng, you obviously haven't assembled the team yet or else you'd have had Mai brought here too and we'd be jetting off to Sankan right now" said Simon.

"Perceptive as always Simon, to answer your question we've assembled half of the team and are en route to New York to recruit the final member" answered Deng as he removed his glasses and placed them in his suit pocket.

"So what are you doing here then?" Simon inquired.

"Honestly I wanted to give you a face to face status update on our deal, and introduce you to one member of the team" answered Deng.

"Where is he?" Simon asked surprised and elated to finally see visible tangible progress.

Deng pointed to the woman standing next to him, "Right here" he said.

Simon looked at Siobhan confused then he looked back at Deng. "You must be out of your damn mind" replied Simon incredulously.

Deng smiled, enjoying Simon's confusion, "Mr. Kane, allow me to introduce Sister Siobhan Costello formerly known as the Devil Woman" answered Deng.

"I prefer to be called The Angel of Vengeance now" said Siobhan.

"Of course you do" said Simon dismissively. Simon had heard of the former IRA assassin named Siobhan Costello and could not believe that this nun before him was her. Every intelligence agency had a file on her, she was a martial arts expert and proficient in almost every kind of firearm known. It was these skills that she used to terrorize England as an enforcer for an ultranationalist splinter cell of the IRA according to her file.

"What are you trying to pull Deng, Siobhan Costello's dead" asked Simon beginning to get more and more annoyed.

"Obviously not" said Deng smugly. Simon looked at the woman again more analytically, She was a very tall, red haired woman with a voluptuous yet muscular body and pale white skin; she was wearing the black and white habit of a catholic nun and wearing a necklace with a golden cross on it. As impossible as it seemed, with the exception of the nun's habit, she matched the description of Siobhan Costello.

"Are you seriously going to tell me that this woman is Siobhan Costello, The Devil Woman?" said Simon skeptically.

"Yes" answered Deng.

Simon sighed and as he pinched the skin above his nose, frustrated with Dengs answers. "Okay assuming she is Siobhan Costello, how the hell is still alive and why is she dressed like a nun?" he inquired.

"Rather than explain myself, I'll let her tell the story" said Deng motioning to Siobhan.

Siobhan took a deep breath as she tried to figure out how to summarize the path her life had taken. "I faked my death and escaped to South America seeking redemption in a convent, eventually I was discovered by Interpol and forced to leave which is when the triad recruited me" she explained.

Simon could tell that there was obviously more to her story as crazy as it sounded.

"I'm curious Mr. Kane, how did you know about me" asked Siobhan.

"I have a friend at MI6 that had several run in's with you he told me all about you" answered Simon.

"I sense you still don't believe this is Siobhan Costello" said Deng.

"What was your first clue?" Simon grunted sarcastically

"Perhaps a test is in order, punch her" Deng continued.

Siobhan and Simon both looked at Deng, there faces a mixture of confusion and surprise. "Now I know you're out of your mind, you want me to punch a nun?" Simon asked.

"What do you want me to do next? Kick a puppy?" said Simon sarcastically.

"What's the problem Simon? If she really is Siobhan Costello then she'll have blocked it before you even know it" said Deng goadingly.

"I don't want to hurt him just to prove a point" Siobhan protested looking down at Deng nervously.

"I wouldn't worry about that Siobhan, Mr. Kane is quite capable" said Deng reassuringly.

"Alright fine, have it your way" sighed Simon as he stood up knowing that either way he was going to regret this. "I just want to make this clear, I'm not the kind of person that hits women" he explained drily.

"You won't" replied Siobhan drily.

"Suit yourself," said Simon shrugged his shoulders. He clenched his fist and threw a punch at Siobhan's head. Almost instantly Siobhan raised her hand and caught the punch with her left hand. Instinctively Simon tried to pull his fist back with all his strength only to discover that she wouldn't let go.

Simon made it a point to exercise every morning and as a result was a very strong man but he couldn't recover his fist from Siobhan's vise of a grip. As he struggled she remained blank and impassive as if Simon's struggling was barely a nuisance to her.

"I said you wouldn't" said Siobhan as Simon continued trying to extricate himself.

Tired of this farce Simon raised his other hand to hit her but to his surprise she caught it. He dug his feet into the floor and pushed and pulled but still couldn't free himself.

"The fuck?" he grunted in surprise.

"You shouldn't curse" replied Siobhan calmly.

He was about to try kicking when she threw him to the floor and before he knew it was on his back. She held his arm against his back and put her weight against him.

"Satisfied?" she asked looking at Deng for an answer.

Deng merely nodded and almost instantly Siobhan let him go and resumed standing as Simon got to his feet and returned to the chair.

"That's a hell of a grip" Simon grunted.

"Do you believe me now?" asked Deng.

"Hard not to, though I have some questions" replied Simon.

"Of course you do but answers are best left for later" Deng explained with a smirk.

Siobhan and Simon looked at Deng somewhat irritated. "If she's part of the team then what is she doing here with you" asked Simon drily.

"Like I said I'm heading to New York to recruit the final member, however we have a…history with the Scarpetta family so I'm using Siobhan as my bodyguard while we're there" answered Deng.

"I'll bet" replied Simon, growing up in New Jersey Simon had heard stories about the Sicilian criminal organization known as the Scarpetta Family, none of them were pleasant. When he joined the CIA he learned the violent details of the "history" Deng mentioned.

"And now Simon, I'm afraid it's time for us to leave" said Deng.

"So it is" said Simon as the two men stood up and walked to the door.

"Where are you and Mai going next?" Deng asked.

"Tangiers, for more of her charity work" answered Simon as the two men shook hands.

"Good Luck" said Deng as Simon walked down the stairs.

"You too" Simon replied.

Deng pushed a button and the door went up and closed. Simon walked back to the car as the plane began to takeoff. Once they were in the air, Siobhan sat down and looked at Deng who was pouring himself a drink. "Well, what did you think?" asked Deng.

Siobhan shrugged, "He's not the stereotypical American, nor is he the revenge crazed madman I was expecting" answered Siobhan.

Deng could tell there was something on her mind that she was hesitant to say. "You have reservations about using him?" asked Deng.

"Deng with all due respect, It's his motivations that concern me" said Siobhan.

"You mean revenge?" said Deng as he sat down.

"Yes, the nuns at the convent had a saying: those who travel the road to revenge tend to get run over" said Siobhan.

Deng smiled at the analogy, "I see, you're concerned that his judgment will be clouded by his deSire for vengeance?"

Siobhan nodded in the affirmative. "I have seen firsthand how revenge can corrupt ones soul"

"You needn't worry, me and the Mountain Master were equally concerned about that but he's proven that our fears were unfounded" said Deng reassuringly.

"I hope you're right" replied Siobhan as she looked out the window.

Chapter 6

Come and Go

Ever since Dennis had met Mack, the other day he had been thinking about his offer. At work he thought about it and while he slept. The last two days had become a blur of bustling activity while Dennis tried to decide: yes or no. He knew there was an endless amount of reasons why he should say no. Aside from the moral reasons there was the fact that if he did accept it he'd be an accessory to murder if he was caught.

Here it was Thursday afternoon in his cubicle at work and he still couldn't decide whether or not to accept Mack's insane offer. However there were plenty of reasons to accept his offer. One such reason was the fact that the book would be a true story and they always sold well. Another reason was that following an assassin around and recording his illicit exploits sounded interesting. Plus as morbid as it sounded, it's not like he would be killing anyone himself he realized.

He leaned back in the chair and laughed secure in the knowledge that no one in his office was thinking about what he was thinking about. At that moment he realized that if he did accept the offer he'd have to leave his apartment and quit his job. This last thought excited him, he had no love for his job and his co-workers barely noticed him, to his bosses he was just another cog in there machine. Then another thought entered his mind could he handle the regret of not accepting the offer and live his life asking himself what if he did accept it. He was a young man in his early twenties so he'd be thinking about it for the rest of his life if he declined the offer.

Did he really want to spend the rest of his life working in this cubicle always wondering about what may have been? Dennis looked around his office at the four cubicle walls claustrophobically surrounding him and knew the answer: No. Dennis reached into his pocket, pulled out his wallet and cellphone. He opened the wallet and pulled out the piece of paper with Mack's phone number on it. Dennis dialed the number on his phone and waited while it rang all the while wondering if he was making a mistake.

After a few rings, a familiar voice answered the phone, Dennis recognized the voice as Macks.

"Hello, who is this" said Mack.

"Mr. Roycewicz my name is Dennis Faraday, we met the other night at the bar" said Dennis feeling kind of stupid.

"Oh…dude, so you in or not?" asked Mack.

"Yeah, I'm in" replied Dennis. "Great I'll pick you up at three tomorrow afternoon" replied Mack.

"Do I need anything like a passport or something" asked Dennis.

"Nah, I got it all taken care of, just be ready when I get there" Mack explained.

"Okay, I'll see you tomorrow at three then" replied Dennis. "Great, bye" said Mack before hanging up.

Dennis retuned his phone and wallet to his pocket while trying to not question his decision. He stood up, grabbed his briefcase and walked out of his cubicle towards the elevator to take a taxi home. As he rode the elevator down to the lobby Dennis considered buying a journal to record information for the book. But he decided against it reasoning that his phone would be better.

******

At around the same time, Deng's plane arrived at JFK airport. They disembarked from the plane and got into a car waiting to take them to a hotel. As they drove through the city Siobhan gazed out the window at the buildings.

"Ever been to New York, Siobhan?" Deng asked.

"No, the only American city I've ever been too was Boston" answered Siobhan while staring out the window.

"I've been there myself, you enjoy it?" Deng asked.

"I wasn't there to visit" Siobhan replied. "What's the plan anyway?" asked Siobhan as she studied the city beyond her window.

"First we notify the Scarpetta Family that we're here, then we track down MAGIC 44" Deng explained.

Siobhan looked back at him confused, "Why do you have to notify them?"

Deng took off his black tea shade sunglasses and sighed "It's a long story" eventually agreed to a treaty that divides the city between us"

"The short version is that it's part of a treaty we have with them whenever we enter their story and vice versa" explained Deng.

"And the long version is?" Siobhan asked.

"Complicated" grunted Deng.

******

Mack arrived at Dennis's apartment at three o'clock on Friday afternoon. He knocked on the door and was greeted by Dennis.

"Ready?" asked Mack.

"Yeah" Dennis replied.

"Great, follow me car's out front" said Mack excitedly.

Dennis followed him out to his parked car; Mack opened the car's trunk and Dennis placed his suitcase in it. The two men then got in the car; Mack sat behind the wheel while Dennis sat next to him and pulled out his phone.

"I'm thinking of using my phone to record information for the book is that alright?" asked Dennis nervously.

"What like World War Z?" asked Mack curiously.

"The movie?" asked Dennis slightly confused.

"No the book" corrected Mack.

"Oh, I see" replied Dennis.

"But yeah that'll be fine" continued Mack.

"Although, I'm going to have to check it when we're done and make sure there's nothing compromising on it, we cool?" said Mack his voice suddenly becoming deadly serious.

"Yes" replied Dennis nervously, feeling slightly afraid for his life. Mack could tell that Dennis was sufficiently intimidated and grinned.

"Great, now relax, we're just going to Canada not North Korea" said Mack dismissively as he started the car and they began driving on their way to JFK airport.

Feeling somewhat reassured Mack pressed the record button on his phone.

"Okay, I gotta ask what's with the Hawaiian shirts?" asked Dennis. Mack looked at him confused.

"What do you mean?" Mack inquired.

"You were wearing one Monday night and you're wearing one now" explained Dennis.

"They're comfortable" Mack answered. Dennis could tell that there was more to it but decided not to press the subject for now at least.

"What's with the tie anyway? We're going to Canada to kill the Spaniel not a wedding, man" continued Mack.

Admittedly Dennis didn't know what to wear to an assassination, he was dressed in gray pants, black tie and a white dress shirt and a gray member's only jacket he fished out of his closet. He was about to admit that Mack had a point when he remembered something Mack said. "Wait, we're going to Canada to kill a Cocker Spaniel?" asked Dennis feeling like he had missed something.

Now it was Mack's time to be confused. "What? No, not a Spaniel, Jimmy the Spaniel and technically I'm going to be killing him" said Mack.

"Who the hell's Jimmy the Spaniel?" asked Dennis, starting to feel agitated by the lack of transparency.

"Jimmy the Spaniel is or was an enforcer for the Scarpetta family till he got greedy and stole 3,000 dollars from them and fled to Canada, so the Scarpetta Family hired me to whack him" answered Mack.

"Oh, why's he called the spaniel" asked Dennis expecting some clichéd mafia story.

"Who the hell knows" replied Mack dismissively.

Chapter 7

Union Man

Upon arriving at the airport Dennis stopped his recording. After going through customs Mack and Dennis were escorted to a private jet on the tarmac. Upon seeing the private jet Dennis's doubts about Mack being an assassin slowly began to erode.

"You coming or not" asked Mack as he boarded the plane. No turning back now thought Dennis as he boarded the plane.

Dennis studied the inside of the plane having never been in a private jet. It resembled a small living room in a fancy hotel room, on one side of the plane was a couch. On the other side were two chairs next to the window with a minibar next to a door that led to what Dennis assumed was the bedroom. Dennis sat down in one of the chairs while Mack went into the cockpit to speak to the pilot. After a few minutes of taxiing the plane barreled down the runway and began to fly.

Once they were in the air, Mack exited the cockpit, "Well, we'll be there in an hour and a half" said Mack as he sat down in the chair next to Dennis.

Dennis pressed record on his cellphone, "I didn't know assassins had private jets" said Dennis half mockingly.

Mack laughed, "I wish it was, it's actually Don Calabresi's plane he loaned it to me for the job, usually I fly first class commercially" replied Mack.

"I have a question" said Dennis.

"Shoot" replied Mack.

"You said the Scarpetta Family hired you to kill this Spaniel guy right?" asked Dennis.

"Uh-huh" replied Mack nonchalantly.

"Why wouldn't they do it themselves instead" asked Dennis.

"Good question, because the Spaniel would expect the Don to send one of his guys, besides for sensitive jobs like this they hire Guild assassins like me" answered Mack.

"Usually they'd make this an open contract for any Guild member, but because I've done work for the Scarpetta family in the past they personally contacted me for the job" he continued.

"What's the Guild?" asked Dennis curiously.

"Very complicated" he replied cryptically.

"Try me" said Dennis.

Mack took a deep breath before answering, so he could figure out how best to explain it. "The best way to explain the Guild is that they are basically a trade union for assassins"

"What do you mean by a "trade union"?" asked Dennis confused.

"They provide members, like me, with jobs, rest, psychological counseling, medical care, supplies, banking and stuff like that" answered Mack.

"And they do this in exchange for?" asked Dennis.

"Protection and a small cut of the money" Mack explained.

"Protection? From who?" asked Dennis even more curious about this organization.

"The Guild has several treaties with each of the world's major criminal organizations which makes the Guild a permanent neutral status but protects them from any attack by allowing them to retaliate and control the fee for contracts" answered Mack.

"Damn" muttered Dennis in shock that something like this could exist.

"I know crazy right" said Mack.

"That's one way of putting it" replied Dennis. Satisfied with the Guild for now

Dennis decided to follow it up with his next question.

"So how do you get a job or a contract?" Dennis asked.

"It depends, but mostly the client sends the Guild a contract and depending on whether it's open or closed the Guild will send it out to every member or to the client's assassin of choice" answered Mack.

"What's the difference between an open contract and a closed contract?" asked Dennis.

"Open contracts are jobs that are available to every member of the Guild, closed contracts are jobs where the client wants a specific member to do the job" Mack answered.

"Although sometimes the client will contact a member directly" continued Mack.

"Like with this job?" asked Dennis. "Bingo" replied Mack.

Dennis took a brief silence to process the enormity of everything and think of his next question. "This all sounds like something out of a movie" said Dennis.

"You'd be surprised how accurate some movies are" replied Mack.

"So, do you always work for the mafia" asked Dennis.

"Not always, but it depends on the job I mostly work for criminal organizations and the occasional revenge jobs, it all depends on where it is though" answered Mack.

"You see I only do jobs in North America, Europe, Asia and occasionally South America" he continued.

"Why?" asked Dennis.

"Because when you do a job in Africa, shit tends to hit the fan like a speeding bullet, plus the jobs in the U.S. and Europe are easier" explained Mack.

"As for the Middle East well...let's just say I had some gnarly experiences there during the war" answered Mack.

Dennis was surprised by the answer, "You were in the war?" asked Dennis.

"Yeah, 75TH Ranger Regiment during the Iraq war" replied Mack.

"Have you ever worked for people like the CIA?" asked Dennis.

Mack laughed at the question much to Dennis's surprise. "That's one thing movies always get wrong, people like the CIA rarely hire Guild members like me"

"Any particular reason?" asked Dennis.

"Too many loose ends for one thing and besides when those spooks do something they do it in house" answered Mack. "Although now that you mention it, there is this urban legend within the Guild involving the Kennedy assassination," he explained.

"Wait, what?" said Dennis surprised.

"Yeah, it's just a rumor but they say someone in the Guild was hired to kill him but nobody knows who" he explained.

"Hey, can we finish the interview tomorrow, I gotta get ready for the job" said Mack.

"Sure" said Dennis as he shrugged his shoulders and stopped recording.

"Great" said Mack as he stood up, "I'll be taking a nap in the bedroom, wake me when we land" said Mack.

Dennis nodded as Mack walked into the bedroom and closed the door behind him. Dennis gazed out the window at the clouds below. What have I gotten myself into. he asked himself.

Chapter 8

The Land of Red Bacon

Dennis knocked on the bedroom door as they landed at Toronto Pearson Airport.

"Sleep well?" asked Dennis as Mack opened the door.

"More or less, I have to talk to the pilot" said Mack.

He turned and walked into the cockpit and spoke to the pilot for a minute. As soon as he exited the cockpit, the plane's door opened and they disembarked the plane only to see a limousine waiting for them on the tarmac.

"It's from the Scarpetta Family, our stuff is already in the trunk" said Mack, Dennis figured as much.

They got in the backseat of the limo and left the airport. "What about the plane?" asked Dennis.

"Don't worry, he'll be taking us back late tonight" answered Mack.

"So where now?" asked Dennis cautiously.

"Now we go to the hotel and get situated" answered Mack.

Dennis couldn't help feel like he was missing something. "What about the Spaniel? Where's he?"

Mack grinned, "Ever been to a Canadian strip club?" asked Mack.

"What?" asked Dennis somewhat floored by the unexpected nature of the question.

"I haven't been in a strip club since college" replied Dennis wondering where Mack was going with this question.

"Ahhh, but you've never been to a Canadian strip club" said Mack clearly enjoying Dennis's confusion.

"What makes Canadian strip clubs better than American ones?" asked Dennis starting to get a little annoyed.

"Canadian strippers" answered Mack.

"What do strippers have to do with Jimmy the Spaniel" asked Dennis.

"He owns a strip club here in Toronto called the Love Muscle" explained Mack.

"Oh, so why didn't you just say that in the first place" asked Dennis annoyed.

"I thought it'd be funny to mess with you" answered Mack chuckling.

Dennis shrugged, while silently admitting to himself that it was kind of funny. "So, what you're just going to walk in there and shoot him with no plan?" he asked.

"Dennis, I'm offended, of course I have a plan" said Mack confidently.

"And that plan is?" asked Dennis.

"Don't worry about it" said Mack.

"I feel like I should" Dennis replied.

"Then you worry too much" replied Mack sarcastically. Before Dennis could respond, they pulled up in front of a large hotel.

"We're here" said Mack as he got out of the car. Dennis and Mack walked around to the trunk and they retrieved their luggage.

"One minute" said Mack as he walked over to the driver's side door and motioned to the driver to lower the window.

Once the window was lowered, "Pick us up here at 8:30" said Mack.

The driver nodded and closed the window before driving away.

"Why so late?" asked Dennis.

"That's when the place really heats up" answered Mack with a grin.

Dennis looked at Mack questioningly.

"What?, might as well enjoy it if we're going there" Mack replied.

The two of them walked into the hotel and checked into a room. Upon entering the room Dennis checked his watch it read: 6:30 pm.

"What do we do for an hour and a half" said Dennis as Mack placed his suitcase on the bed.

"We'll find something to do, I know a great Steakhouse down the street" answered Mack while he opened his suitcase.

Dennis glanced inside and saw just clothes and a plastic bag with a toothbrush and toothpaste in it. Suddenly Dennis realized something, "Where's your gun?" he asked.

"At home in New York" replied Mack drily.

"Why didn't you bring it?" asked Dennis confused, "I didn't bring them because if I did we wouldn't be able to get into the Love Muscle" answered Mack.

"Then how are you going to kill him" Dennis asked.

"I'll figure it out when we get there" answered Mack confidently.

"I thought you had a plan" Dennis complained.

"I do, my plan is to improvise" replied Mack.

"That's not much of a plan" said Dennis with a sigh, still confused while Mack finished checking his suitcase.

"Wanna get something to eat" asked Mack.

"Sure" replied Dennis.

Chapter 9

The Messenger

By the time they finished eating dinner it was seven fifty-five, they left the restaurant and walked back to the hotel room. "So now what?" asked Dennis?

"Now we go back to the hotel get our stuff do the job and go home" answered Mack.

"Why bring your stuff at all then?" asked Dennis.

"Honestly, I like to be prepared" answered Mack. Upon returning to the hotel they picked up there stuff and checked out. By the time they were finished, the limo was parked in front of the hotel. They put their luggage in the limo's trunk and got in the backseat of the limo.

"You know where to go" said Mack, the driver nodded in response then started the car.

Outside it was dark, the only lights coming from the buildings around them, in the distance loomed the CN tower like some all seeing eye. After driving for an hour, they arrived at the Love Muscle. In front of the door was a large bald man acting as the bouncer. They parked across the street from the Love Muscle.

"Here's a little extra if you wait for us" said Mack as he handed the driver two fifty dollar bills.

"Let's rock it" said Mack to Dennis as he got out of the car.

Dennis followed him across the street wondering how they were going to get in. Mack approached the bouncer.

"Welcome Sir, who's he?" said the bouncer pointing to Dennis. "Oh him, he's a friend" said Mack dismissively.

"Very well Sir" said the bouncer as he stepped aside.

As they walked into the Love Muscle Dennis could swear that he saw the bouncer pull a phone out of his suit jacket and start talking on it. Once inside the Love Muscle they were greeted by a cacophony of light and sound. The whole strip club was bathed in pink overhead lights with music playing in speakers overhead. On the left side of the strip club was the bar. On the other side were three run-way like stages with gorgeous scantily clad women pole dancing on them. In the middle of the bar and the stages were tables and chairs filled with people and half naked waitresses delivering drinks.

"Welcome to the Love Muscle" said Mack.

"Nice place" said Dennis as he took the place in.

"C'mon let's get a drink" said Mack.

Dennis shrugged and followed Mack over to a booth and they sat down.

"Told you this place was awesome!" yelled Mack over the blaring music.

"What?!" replied Dennis, before Mack could answer two large men in suits walked up to their table.

"The boss would like to speak with you" said one of them.

Mack got up and motioned to Dennis to follow him.

"Lead the way" said Mack. They followed the two men out of the club and up a short flight of stairs.

As they followed them, Mack turned and looked over at Dennis his face dead serious. "Don't say a damn thing" hissed Mack.

Dennis nodded suddenly feeling a little scared, at the top of the stairs was a hallway with a door at the end of it. The men stopped and turned to face Mack and Dennis.

"We have to pat you down" said one of them.

"Go on" said Mack as he held out his arms. Dennis followed suit, after a brief pat down one of them opened the door and they walked inside the office. It was a dimly lit office room with closed circuit televisions against the wall behind a desk. In front of the desk were two chairs. Seated behind the desk was a short, skinny ugly man in a suit with black slicked back hair and a pencil thin mustache.

"Hey Jimmy, it's been awhile" said Mack politely.

"Yes it has, sit down please" said Jimmy, Mack and Dennis sat down in the two chairs in front of the desk.

"Love the club, Jimmy" Mack said.

"What are you doing here Mack?" said Jimmy.

"Oh, well, me and my friend here were in town and I heard about this place from Achille so I figured we'd check it out" said Mack jovially.

"Is that a fact?" asked Jimmy as he opened a desk drawer.

"What else could it be?" replied Mack smugly. Suddenly Jimmy pulled out a small revolver and aimed it at them, his face livid with rage.

"Do I look like a fucking idiot you mother fucker?" barked Jimmy.

"Depends on what kind of fucking idiot, I hear there's a lot" replied Mack drily.

Dennis sat there paralyzed with fear, in that moment he realized that this wasn't just some elaborate joke, this was real.

Jimmy stood up slowly, "Don Calabresi hired you to come here and kill me didn't he" said Jimmy smugly as he walked around the table and stood next to Mack.

"What, nooo" said Mack sarcastically, "Jimmy think about it if he did hire me to kill you then wouldn't I have brought a gun with me?" said Mack.

"I don't believe you" Jimmy said as he pulled back the hammer on the revolver and held it right against Mack's ear.

"Well that's too bad" said Mack sighing.

Suddenly Mack hit Jimmy in the stomach with his elbow Jimmy's gun with his left hand causing him to drop the gun. Jimmy knelt in pain while Mack jumped to his feet and backhanded Jimmy in the face knocking him to the floor. Mack knelt down and picked up the gun just as the two guards burst into the office, guns drawn. Mack swung around and shot one of them in the head and then the other one. Mack shifted his attention back to Jimmy, who was lying on his back. Mack aimed the revolver at his head, Jimmy held up his hands weakly.

"We can make a deal please don't kill me" pleaded Jimmy.

Mack sighed, "Sorry man, look if it was up to me I'd let you go but I've already been paid and honestly you brought this on yourself" said Mack. He pulled the trigger and in an instant the light in Jimmy the Spaniel's eyes departed. Dennis sat in the chair feeling equal parts horrified and in shock. With the exception of the blaring music from the club downstairs the room became dead silent. The silence was interrupted by Dennis vomiting on the floor. "Nasty" said Mack looking over, "You okay?" asked Mack.

"Am I okay? Are you okay? You fucking killed them!?" yelled Dennis, his voice palpable with terror and outrage. "Well...yeah, I told you I'm an assassin" said Mack calmly and defensively.

"Jesus, that's not the point and why the hell are you so calm about this?" barked Dennis.

"Please do you have any idea how many times I've had a gun pointed at me, honestly it's not a big deal" replied Mack dismissively as he slid the gun into his pants pocket.

"Now do you want to stay here or do you want to wait for the cops" continued Mack as he walked out the door.

Sensing little recourse Dennis followed Mack out of the office trying not to look at the dead body on the floor behind him. As they walked through the club the people were oblivious to what happened upstairs. The music must have drowned out the sound of the gunshots realized Dennis. Upon returning to the limo, they drove back to the airport. Mack pulled his cellphone out of his pocket and started texting. "What the hell are you doing?" asked Dennis as if in a daze.

"Notifying the Guild that I fulfilled the contract" answered Mack.

"Then they'll notify the Scarpetta Family right" Dennis replied.

"Bingo, see now you're getting it" answered Mack.

"So now what, back to New York?" asked Dennis.

"Yep, then straight from the airport to see the Don" Mack answered.

"Right the Don....Wait what?" said Dennis.

"Yeah the Don of the Scarpetta Family" replied Mack casually, as he put the phone in his pocket.

Chapter 10

Person of Interest

"Tā mā de!" muttered Deng as he ended the phone call.

"Something wrong?" asked Siobhan drolly as she sat at the table reading a magazine.

"Ever since we got here I've been sending people all over New York trying to find MAGIC 44" said Deng as he returned the phone to his pocket.

"And they found nothing?" said Siobhan not looking up from the magazine.

"Yes, to my continued annoyance" answered Deng.

"The lord helps those who wait" Siobhan replied casually.

Deng ignored the remark and sat at the table across from her looking considerably annoyed. "Why is he called MAGIC 44 anyway?" asked Siobhan.

"It's Guild protocol that every member be assigned a codename" answered Deng dismissively.

"Where the hell is he?" muttered Deng, suddenly Deng's phone rang loudly. Deng hurriedly pulled out the phone and answered it. "Who is this?" asked Deng, he was silent for a few seconds. "I see, yes we'll be there immediately" said Deng his look of annoyance having been replaced with satisfaction.

Siobhan looked up from her magazine as Deng ended the call. "Who was that?" she asked

"The leader of the Scarpetta Family, Don Calabresi" Deng answered as he stood up and walked to the closet.

"What did he want?" asked Siobhan curiously.

"He wants to meet us at the restaurant across the street" answered Deng as he pulled his black trench coat out of the closet and put it on.

Siobhan sighed as she put down the magazine and reached for her gun holster.

"No guns" said Deng as she reached for it, Siobhan shrugged and followed Deng out of the room to the elevator. Upon reaching the elevator at the end of the hallway Deng pushed the down button and they waited a few seconds for it to come.

"What do they want to see us for?" asked Siobhan as they rode the elevator down from the ninth floor.

"I don't know, probably to ask some questions" Deng answered.

"What am I supposed to do then?" asked Siobhan.

"What I brought you here for: to be my bodyguard" replied Deng.

When they arrived at the lobby they walked out the door across the street to the restaurant. The restaurant was called Le Blanco and was filled with the well to do of the city. Deng and Siobhan approached the maitre de standing behind a podium in the front of the restaurant.

"We've been expecting you two, the rest of your party is waiting in the private dining room follow me" said the headwaiter smugly. They followed him across the dining room, the patrons staring at them as trying to figure out what business a Chinese man and nun were doing together. Upon arriving at the door to the private dining room, the headwaiter opened it and they walked inside. The room was fairly large with a single table in the middle with three men in suits eating.

Two of the men were much younger and were wearing bowling shirts.

While the man sitting between them was much older, the older man had slicked back white hair and was wearing a red dress shirt with a black tie, vest, pants and suit jacket. Siobhan assumed that he must be Don Calabresi and the two younger men in bowling shirts were his bodyguards. When they walked in the three men looked up confused.

"Ciao" Deng said drily.

"Shin" grunted Don Calabresi in return.

"It's actually Shen" corrected Deng.

"My apologies" said Don Calabresi disingenuously. "I hear you have a problem" continued Don Calabresi.

"I don't know where you heard that" said Deng as he sat down at the table across from the three men.

Siobhan sat next to him, "What's with the nun? You find Jesus?" said the older man gesturing to Siobhan with his fork.

"She's my bodyguard, Don Calabresi" answered Deng bluntly. Calabresi's two bodyguards snickered at Deng's answer.

"You think God will protect you?" asked Don Calabresi smugly.

"Depends on the God" replied Deng sarcastically, for the next few seconds both men were silent.

"Right, see that's why I like this guy" laughed Don Calabresi. "Got a real a sense of humor at least for a Japanese" continued Don Calabresi.

"I'm Chinese" corrected Deng, feeling somewhat insulted.

"There a difference?" asked Don Calabresi dismissively.

"Plenty unlike Italians and Sicilians" said Deng with a smug smile.

"Watch your mouth when speaking to the Boss!" barked one of the bodyguards as he stood up and approached Deng preparing to strike him. Before he could strike him Siobhan jumped up and kicked him in the back of his left leg then placed him in a full nelson. The other bodyguard jumped up quickly to aid his comrade. Don Calabresi held up his hand and the guard stopped and sat back down. The Don stared at Deng for a minute and then started laughing.

"Italians and Sicilians…that's a good one" said Don Calabresi.

"I knew you'd appreciate it, now tell me why you wanted to see me?" said Deng.

"Release him first" said Don Calabresi.

Deng looked at Siobhan and nodded, she released the bodyguard and he fell to the floor imbibing in great gulps of air. He stood up, his face filled with rage, turned to face Siobhan preparing to strike her.

"Gino siediti ora!" barked the Don before he could hit her. The man stopped as the look of livid rage departed his face and he returned to his seat.

"Le mie scuse Don Calabresi" whispered Gino.

"Allow me to apologies my bodyguards, Gino and Carmine, are young and hot blooded" Don Calabresi said.

"Now like I said we heard you have a little problem, a little problem named MAGIC 44" said Don Calabresi.

"How did you know?" asked Deng curiously.

"After I was notified that you were here I got curious so I had my people look into it" answered the Don.

"I see. So of what interest is MAGIC 44 to you?" Deng asked.

"I could ask you the same thing" said Don Calabresi.

"We need him for something" answered Deng.

Don Calabresi shrugged, "You're not going to tell me what it is you want him for are you?" continued Don Calabresi.

"If you were in my position would you?" replied Deng.

"Fair enough" said Don Calabresi.

"Do you know where he is?" asked Deng.

Don Calabresi sighed as he checked his watch. "By now he should be on his way back from Toronto"

"I see, well then I think we're finished here" said Deng.

"Actually no we're not" said Don Calabresi.

"Oh" said Deng inquisitively.

"Yes, ever since we signed that peace treaty years ago there hasn't been a single conflict between our organizations here in New York" said Don Calabresi.

"Your point" said Deng impatiently.

"My point is that I want an assurance that whatever it is you need MAGIC 44 for won't affect my organization" answered Don Calabresi sounding more than a little annoyed.

"You can rest assured that it won't affect you in any way" said Deng as he and Siobhan stood up to leave.

"Addio Don Calabesi" said Deng before they walked out of the room and returned to the hotel.

"Sir, do you believe him" asked Gino.

"No, but I want him kept under surveillance as long as they're in New York" answered Don Calabresi.

"Then why tell him about MAGIC 44" asked the bodyguard.

"Because the sooner they find him the sooner he goes back to that damn island of his" answered Don Calabresi.

"And what about MAGIC 44? How do you want to deal with him" asked the bodyguard.

"For now leave him alone, though perhaps he's become a bit of a liability to the family" said Don Calabresi before taking a sip of wine from the bottle in front of him.

Chapter 11

The Finger on the Trigger

Whenever Dennis closed his eyes all he could see was the death of Jimmy the Spaniel over and over again like a nightmare without end. As he slept on the plane he kept reliving that scene over and over again. When the gun went off he woke up and after a few seconds remembered where he was.

"Sleep well?" asked Mack disinterestedly.

Dennis turned around and saw him standing behind the bar pouring himself a glass of water. "Not really, where are we?" Dennis asked weakly.

"Almost home" said Mack as he walked over to the small refrigerator and got a bottled water.

"Here, you look thirsty" said Mack as he handed Dennis the bottle. As he drank the water Mack sat down in the chair across from him.

"I know how you feel" said Mack somberly as he drank some of the water in his glass. Dennis looked at him quizzically.

"The shock, the horror, the fear, the first one I ever killed was some kid in Afghanistan when I was in the Rangers" said Mack tiredly.

Dennis looked up at him a horrified look on his face. "It's not what you think, he was running at me with an AK about to shoot" said Mack. Dennis's look of horror subsided somewhat at Mack's answer.

"It's funny, they can teach you all the ways to kill but not how to deal with it" said

Mack looking out the window at the clouds beyond.

"How do you handle it?" Dennis asked.

"Well I can't speak for other members but the Guild's shrinks recommend we get a hobby to help take our minds off the job" Mack answered.

"What's yours then?" asked Dennis.

"Well…ever since I was a kid I've liked comic books and movies, so in my free time I basically read and collect comic books, watch movies and anime y'know nerd shit" replied Mack.

"Huh" Dennis grunted in mild surprise.

"What?" said Mack defensively.

"Nothing, I just didn't expect you to say comic books and movies were your hobby" said Dennis.

"What did you expect me to say?" Mack replied.

"I don't know, like gardening or something" answered Dennis.

"Gardening? Do I look like the Professional to you?" replied Mack sarcastically.

Dennis thought for a minute trying to figure out what he meant. Suddenly he remembered that the Professional was a movie. "Well no, I don't remember much about that movie but I don't recall him wearing Hawaiian Shirts either" said Dennis with a grin.

Mack laughed, "Well yeah, that just means I'm a better dresser"

"Why do you do this?" asked Dennis in frustration. It was a question that had been burning within him ever since he woke up.

"What?" asked Mack.

"Why do you have to live this way? Killing people for money?" clarified Dennis.

Mack looked at him harshly as if he was insulted by the question. "First: When I got out of the Army, I couldn't get a job, I was homeless until these mobsters paid me five hundred bucks to kill someone they didn't like" answered Mack sternly.

"Second: I only kill the people that I feel deserve it" Mack continued.

"Third, and this is the important part because it separates us from serial killers, we have a code" finished Mack.

Dennis decided not to press the issue any further but he was intrigued by the mention of a code and rules.

"What do you mean by a code?" asked Dennis.

"Well the Guild has their own rules that you have to comply with" explained Mack

"And what happens to those that don't follow the rules?" asked Dennis, already having a good idea about the answer.

"Well…they lose their membership and depending on the infractions they're terminated" answered Mack.

"I see, and what are these rules?" asked Dennis.

"There's only three: the Guild gets a small percentage of money from each job a member does, No business is conducted at the Guilds facilities and members can't accept a contract on any American politicians" answered Mack.

"Why?" asked Dennis perplexed.

Mack shrugged, "no one knows, but that and the lounges neutrality are the only rules the Guild has" answered Mack.

"What about the code?" asked Dennis.

"It's not official it's just a credo we have, avoid collateral damage as much as possible, use precision and professionalism, always get paid and no contracts on children" answered Mack.

"What about women?" Dennis asked confused, since he expected him to say no women or children.

"What about them?" asked Mack confused at the question.

"Why aren't women under the same protection as children?" clarified Dennis.

Mack laughed loudly making Dennis feel like he was missing something. "What's so funny?" asked Dennis slightly annoyed.

"Sorry for laughing, but just think about it women can be just as lethal, sadistic and dangerous as men can" answered Mack.

"Hell, in some ways they're even more dangerous than men" continued Mack.

"How?" asked Dennis, "It depends but I think it's for two reasons, number one: your average vic doesn't expect to be killed by a woman" answered Mack.

"They usually expect it to be a dude like me or something" Mack continued.

Dennis assumed "vic" must be slang for an assassin's target. Once again the bleeding body of Jimmy the Spaniel flashed through his mind, Dennis shivered at the thought barely noticeably.

"Secondly, It's because depending on the woman they can use their appearance and sex as a weapon of deception like a Trojan Horse or a Bond girl to get in close" said Mack.

"Basically no one's going to expect to get whacked by a hot chick to kill them" continued Mack.

"Interesting theory" said Dennis as he thought about it.

"It's not a theory man, hell I know a couple Guild members that are women and they're scary as shit" replied Mack.

"Really?" asked Dennis.

"Yeah the scariest one, at least that I've met, is this one chick: KATYUSHA" continued Mack.

"KATYUSHA?" asked Dennis.

"Yeah it's a codename, every Guild assassin is assigned a codename for classification" answered Mack.

"What's yours?" asked Dennis curiously, "MAGIC 44" answered Mack.

"Why MAGIC 44?" Dennis queried.

"What?" asked Mack noticing a look of surprise on Dennis's face.

"Nothing, it's just not what I was expecting I mean it sounds like a band or something" replied Dennis.

"Hey I didn't pick it besides I'd listen to it as long as it isn't country" protested Mack.

Dennis shrugged, deciding to change the subject. "So…this KATYUSHA, what else can you tell me about her?" asked Dennis.

"I don't think you're her type, Dennis" answered Mack grinning.

For a split second Dennis thought he was serious but then realized it was a joke and laughed mildly.

"She's Russian, her first name is Sasha I think she used to work for the FSB or the SVR or something, she usually works in the Middle East, Africa and Asia" said Mack. "Oh one other thing she wears an eye patch over her right eye and she is smoking hot dude" explained Mack.

"An eye patch what happened to her eye?" asked Dennis, Mack shrugged his shoulders.

"Don't know, One thing I do know though, the only woman deadlier than her is the Devil Woman" Mack said.

"Who's the Devil Woman?" asked Dennis.

"She wasn't a Guild member but she was an assassin for the IRA, from what I've heard she was this badass hardcore super-terrorist that could go head to head with the British SAS and Navy SEALS combined and win" continued Mack.

"Come on?" asked Dennis not believing his claims.

"Rumor is she took out an entire SAS unit with a paper clip" said Mack.

"How do you kill someone with a paper clip?" Dennis asked.

"Fuck if I know, that's just what I heard so take it with a grain of salt" said Mack dismissively.

"What happened to her?" asked Dennis.

"Like all terrorists she got cocky and tried to blow up Balmoral castle with a car bomb and the guards stopped her dead before she could get too close" explained Mack.

"In the end she was just like every other terrorist a mad dog that got put down" said Mack.

"How do you reconcile the actions of this Devil Woman with yours which could be considered terrorist" asked Dennis afraid that he might be offended by the question.

"That's a good question, I suppose the only real difference is that I kill for money and people like her kill for ideology" answered Mack.

"Besides I don't kill innocent people…that and I don't work for terrorists no Guild assassin does…well the crazy ones do" continued Mack.

"Why?" asked Dennis.

"Well technically there's nothing to say you can't it's just the Guild discourages it since terrorists can be unreliable when it comes to paying" Mack answered.

"And how much does a job cost?" asked Dennis.

"It depends, the Guild sets the prices based on the degree of difficulty involved and the status of the target among other things however you can name your own price as long as the Guild gets its cut" answered Mack.

"But to answer your question payment can be anything from a couple thousand to a million" Mack continued.

"So that's how much a human life is worth" said Dennis cynically.

"Hey man, its business" shrugged Mack.

"So how much does the Guild get from a contract?" asked Dennis.

"Again it depends on the job's price but for the most part they take like fifteen or twenty percent" answered Mack. Suddenly he snapped his fingers, "I just got an idea" said Mack mildly excited.

"You've been asking about the Guild and other Guild members, well how about I introduce you to a few" continued Mack.

"What?" said Dennis.

"C'mon it'll be fun, might help with the book" said Mack exuberantly.

"What about meeting with the Don?" asked Dennis.

"He won't be expecting us for a few hours so we'll have some time to kill" said Mack.

Suddenly Dennis realized that he hadn't recorded their conversation on the phone. He decided against telling Mack besides if he was telling the truth he would probably never forget this whole ordeal.

*****

Meanwhile in New York at Don Calabresi's Mansion on Long Island Don Calabresi sat at a meeting with his personal Consigliere, Vito Messana, and the Underboss of the Scarpetta Family, Frank Basso. For the past hour Don Calabresi had been sitting at the table describing his meeting with Deng.

"Gentlemen, what do you think?" asked Don Calabresi.

"I don't like it" said Messana "None of us do" said Don Calabresi.

"Why don't we just whack this Deng guy and be done with it" said Basso.

"We do that and we go to war with the triad and the Vasilev Syndicate, remember the treaty" said Don Calabresi.

There was no need for a spoken answer, the treaty that ended hostilities between them and the triad was like ashes in their mouths.

"We could make it look like an accident" protested Basso.

"They'd know it was us since we're the only enemies they have in New York we'd be an instant suspect" said Messana.

"You got any other ideas?" barked Basso.

"Yes, put out an open contract on Mack and let the Guild take care of it for us" said Messana.

"Are you insane? That man has helped us for years and you want to stab him in the back?" protested Basso adamantly.

"We have to confront the possibility that the triad might use him against us since they know he's worked for us in the past" Messana continued.

"I hate to admit it but he's right mercenaries like Mack are loyal to money and money alone" said Don Calabresi.

Basso was about to voice an objection but Don Calabresi raised his hand and Basso went silent.

Chapter 12

Over and Under

An hour later Mack and Dennis arrived at JFK airport, after disembarking the plane they walked through the terminal and to the parking lot where Mack's car was parked. After getting in the car, Mack turned the key and started the engine and backed out of the parking lot. "So where we going?" asked Dennis.

Mack gave him a surprised look, "to meet some buddies of mine" answered Mack as they drove away from the airport.

"You were serious about that?" said Dennis surprised.

"Duh" replied Mack smugly.

"Alright, but where are we going to meet these people" asked Dennis.

"You'll see, besides you've been there before" said Mack.

"I have?" said Dennis curiously.

"Yep, by the way I recommend that you leave your phone in the car" answered Mack.

"Got it" said Dennis tensely.

"Dude, relax they won't kill you," Mack said casually.

"You sure?" Dennis asked. "Probably" replied Mack with a shrug.

"Well that's reassuring" said Dennis sarcastically.

After almost forty-five minutes of driving through the meandering streets of Manhattan they arrived at a familiar liquor establishment. "What are we doing at Carlitos?" Dennis asked confused.

"You'll see" said Mack as he parked the car in a small lot behind the bar.

This makes no sense why are we back here thought Dennis. When the car came to a stop they got out, Dennis made sure to leave his phone in the car. In front of them was the rear of the bar made out of brick; to their left right and back were three buildings.

"So now what" asked Dennis impatiently.

"Now? Now you see something cool" Mack replied.

He pulled out his cellphone and aimed it at the back door of the bar and pressed a few buttons there was a barely audible beeping and then the door slid to the side like a sliding door in its place was an elevator door. On the right side of the elevator was a small rectangular section of brick wall slid that suddenly slid to the side revealing a console. Mack walked up to the console and placed his hand on a green square in the middle of the console then looked into a small electric eye.

After a few seconds there were a few beeps and the elevator doors opened. Mack stepped back from the console as the panel slid over the console. He gestured to the open elevator, "after you" said Mack.

Dennis shrugged and walked inside, it's too late to turn back now he thought. Mack walked in after him and the doors closed in front of them. The interior of the elevator looked like the elevator in an office building. Mack pushed a button next to the door with a white arrow on it. Instantly the elevator began to go down into the Earth.

"So where are we going? The Bat Cave" asked Dennis.

"Nah, this place is much roomier" said Mack looking like he was waiting for a bus. Suddenly the elevator stopped and the doors opened into a short white hallway. In the middle of the hallway's ceiling, left and right walls were small black dome shaped objects.

"What are those black things?" asked Dennis.

"Yeah I forgot about this part, we got to go through security, those'll scan you from head to toe for anything dangerous" answered Mack.

"Right" replied Dennis.

Mack walked out of the elevator and down the hall nonchalantly. Sensing little recourse Dennis followed him to the end of the hall. Once they reached the end of the hall was the door at the other end opened. They walked into what appeared to be a lobby with a few wooden chairs a table and a carpet. On one of the walls was a window with a counter beneath it; behind the window was a surly looking bald man dressed in black. The only thing out of place in the room was the giant reinforced steel door on the other side. Dennis followed Mack over to the window.

"Que Pasa" asked Mack politely.

The man scowled at him in response. He looked at a computer screen then back at Mack and Dennis.

"MAGIC 44, scans show you are not carrying any weapons" said the man.

"Your point?" asked Mack sounding a little annoyed.

"You may pass" replied the man.

"The man with you, according to the computer his name is Dennis Faraday a former employee of Minute Broadcasting is also unarmed" said the man dispassionately.

Dennis suddenly became tense. Those scanners must have identified me he thought. He was not surprised to have been fired but was still unnerved by how they could instantly identify him like that. "Why is he here?" asked the man.

"He's a friend of mine, look I'll vouch for him alright" Mack said.

The man behind the glass looked at Dennis studiously. His gaze returned to Mack. "Since you are a member in good standing, with no strikes against you, he may enter just be aware that any rules he breaks will apply to you" said the man as he pushed a red button on the keyboard in front of him.

"It pays to behave" grunted Mack drily. Instantly the giant steel door slid open revealing another elevator with the doors already open.

"Thanks" Mack replied before walking into the elevator with Dennis following him. He pushed a button marked L on the console and the elevator doors closed.

"You wanna tell me what that was all about?" asked Dennis.

"Security measures! Can't be too careful in this line of work" Mack answered. Dennis looked at him confused. "Dude we're assassins not serial killers" protested Mack.

"Of course, so I'm assuming the bar above us is a cover right?" asked Dennis.

"Bingo" replied Mack.

"So where we going now?" asked Dennis pleased that he managed to figure something out for himself in the last few days.

"The real Carlitos" replied Mack.

Before Dennis could ask for clarification the elevator doors opened and they found themselves in a large dimly lit room. There were red chairs and wooden tables in the center of the room with people sitting in them talking. Up against the wall were red booths with wood tables in front of them. On the other side of the room was a bar with a bartender behind it serving drinks. Playing softly from the ceiling on loudspeakers was smooth jazz music. Dennis followed Mack to a booth on the other side of the room some of the people inside glanced at them. Upon sitting down Dennis looked around the room incredulously. "How do you guys maintain something like this?" he asked.

"We don't, the Guild does using the money they take from us plus they get donations from various criminal organizations" Mack explained.

"Amazing" said Dennis. "Tell me about it, hey you want something to drink?" asked Mack.

"Water" replied Dennis.

"Got it, be right back" said Mack as he stood up and walked to the bar.

While Mack was at the bar getting the drinks Dennis looked around the room studying some of the people inside. There were around twelve people in the room all busy talking or on their cellphones. However, at the far end of the room, seated in a corner covered were two men with identical faces that were dressed in black dress shirts and pants. One of them had a Red tie the other wore a purple tie. They just sat there staring at everyone in the room. Dennis shifted his gaze from them to Mack who was walking back to the table with two glasses in his hands.

"Here's your water" said Mack as he handed the glass to Dennis and sat down.

"Thanks, what are you drinking?" asked Dennis before he took a sip of water from his glass.

"Ginger Ale" answered Mack.

"Right, hey what's up with those two over there?" Dennis asked as he pointed at the two staring men.

Mack looked over to see who he was pointing at and then back at Dennis.

"Oh those two, yeah they're the Razzle Dazzle twins" answered Mack.

"Any reason they're called that?" asked Dennis.

"Their real names are Razlov and Dazlov, so my guess is that has something to do with it" said Mack.

"Which ones which?" asked Dennis.

"I don't know, I'll tell you this though those two creep me out so I avoid them like the plague" continued Mack.

"I can see why" said Dennis noticing that they were still staring laconically at everyone in the room. "So...is this the Guild's only bar?" he asked.

"Hell no, there's six of them hidden across the world for the Guilds members" answered

Mack who followed the answer with a gulp of ginger ale.

"Who runs all of this?" asked Dennis as Mack leaned back in his chair.

"No one knows, hell no one even knows who runs the Guild, I've heard rumors that it's someone called Progenitore, but no one knows his real name" answered Mack.

"How can you not know?" asked Dennis.

"Dude, it's not just me, no one knows who runs this shit or how it even got started," said Mack.

"Do you have any ideas?" Dennis asked.

"To be honest with you I never really thought about it" Mack replied. "For all I know it could be the damn CIA" he said dismissively.

"Does anyone know about this?" asked Dennis.

"What you mean like the cops?" replied Mack.

Dennis nodded. "Nah, no one does and those that do are either paid well for their silence, have bad memories or don't care" said Mack.

Before Dennis could ask another question an Asian man of medium height walked over to them. He stood in front of their table intimidatingly. There was an angry look in his eyes as he looked at Mack. He was dressed in a white dress shirt, long black pants, black tie, red vest with brown shoes and a white fedora.

"Hey STROBE, how're things?" asked Mack nicely.

"You know damn well how "things" are 44" said the man irritably.

"And who the hell is this?" continued the man as he pointed to Dennis.

"Friend of mine, his names Dennis" said Mack.

"I don't care who he is, why is he here?" answered the man.

"Because he's thirsty, and it's not against the rules for him to be here" answered Mack.

"Fine, just watch it" growled the man before walking back to his table.

"What's his problem?" asked Dennis.

"His names Sato Masaki codename: STROBE, used to run with the Yamaguchi-gumi then he went freelance" explained Mack.

"The hell is the Yamaguchi-gumi?" asked Dennis having never heard the words before. "One of the The Yakuza" answered Mack. "A year ago I beat him to a contract and he's held a grudge ever since" continued Mack.

"That's gotta put you on edge" said Dennis.

"Not really, guy's like him live by the sword and die by the sword know what I mean" answered Mack.

"And you?" asked Dennis.

"Me? I don't have that problem you see I try to leave emotion out of it, if I miss a job I miss a job no worry" answered Mack before taking another gulp of Ginger Ale.

"That's a very cavalier attitude" replied Dennis. "Call it what you will, I call it perspective, if you lose it you lose" said Mack.

"That's very profound" said Dennis sarcastically.

Suddenly the large steel door they entered the lounge through opened and through it walked a tall woman with blonde hair. She was dressed in black pants, red boots, red sweater and a black leather jacket. She was attractive enough to be a supermodel except for the black eye patch covering her right eye.

"No freakin way" said Mack as the woman walked to the bar and ordered a drink.

"What?" asked Dennis.

"That's the Russian woman I told you about earlier" said Mack as he pointed to her.

Dennis thought carefully for a minute as he tried to remember her name. "You mean KATYUSHA?" asked Dennis, at the mention of her name the woman finished her drink and walked over to their table.

"Hey Sasha, I heard about that job you did in Sankan a few months ago" said Mack when she approached them.

"Yes, it was difficult job but jobs for the Vasilev Syndicate usually are, who is this man?" said Sasha gesturing to Dennis.

She spoke in a thick Russian accent that was both seductive and threatening at the same time. Dennis was starting to get irritated at being referred to as an outsider but he was more confused by what Sankan was.

"This is a friend of mine, his names Dennis" said Mack, Sasha held out her hand.

"Privet" said Sasha as Dennis and her shook hands.

"So what are you doing here?" asked Mack.

"My connecting flight to Marrakesh leaves tomorrow morning" she answered.

"Still looking for Aquarius?" asked Mack.

"Yes, I'll see you later there's some people here I must talk to, I'll see you later" said Sasha as she walked away.

"Crazy coincidence right?" said Mack looking back at Dennis grinning.

"What's Sankan?" asked Dennis. "The worst place in the world" answered Mack ominously.

"And Aquarius?" asked Dennis, before Mack could answer the bartender walked up to them with an envelope.

"Excuse me gentlemen, this just came for you" said the bartender as he handed Mack the envelope. Mack nodded at him in appreciation and he walked back to the bar. Mack shifted his attention back to the envelope. He studied the envelope quickly then opened it and pulled out a letter. "Huh" grunted Mack in mild surprise as he read the letter.

"Well?" asked Dennis inquisitive about the letter.

"Don Calabresi wants to see me" answered Mack.

The sheer unexpectedness of the invitation blindsided Dennis putting him at a loss for words. "Wanna come?" asked Mack nonchalantly.

Dennis thought for a minute if going to a meeting between a mob boss and an assassin was a good idea. Then again he knew that so far everything he had done with Mack could be considered a bad idea and that it was too late to back out now.

"Sure, what could go wrong?" replied Dennis.

Mack grinned ever so slightly. "Alright then, let's go" he said as he stood up.

"What, you mean now?" asked Dennis surprised.

"Yeah, there's a car waiting for us upstairs" answered Mack.

"Of course there is" muttered Dennis as he stood up and followed Mack out of the bar.

Chapter 13

The Big Boss

After driving for two hours they arrived at Don Calabresi's mansion in Long Island. It was an opulent beachfront mansion with a brick façade, and what Dennis assumed were two floors located on a lonely stretch of road. As they pulled up to the mansion Dennis leaned over to Mack who was seated next to him in the backseat of the limo.

"I thought the mafia was wiped out?" whispered Dennis.

"Nah, they just went underground" responded Mack.

Before Dennis could ask a follow up question they stopped in the front parking lot. Instinctively they stepped out of the car and were greeted by a man in a black and white suit. "Before you can come inside I have to check you both for any weapons" said the man.

"Go ahead, we're clean" said Mack as he held out his arms, Dennis decided to follow suit.

The man patted them down, checking for weapons. "Good, come with me" said the man, he turned around and opened the door.

Mack and Dennis followed him inside, Dennis felt like he was walking through Buckingham palace. In the center of the mansion was a staircase they followed the man up the staircase and down a hallway. At the end of the hall were two wooden double doors. Upon arriving at the doors, the man turned around to face them. "He's waiting for you inside" said the man as he gestured to the door.

Mack leaned over to Dennis closely so the other man couldn't hear what he was about to say. "I'll do the talking, got it?" he whispered.

Dennis nodded in understanding and Mack backed away from him as the man opened the door. Dennis followed Mack into the room as the man closed the large wooden doors behind them. The carpeted room was dominated by a lit fireplace; in front of it was a wooden table, a black reclining chair and a red couch on the other side of the table.

The air was rich with the acidic scent of cigar smoke, the black chair swung around to face them. Reclining in the chair was Don Calabresi. An older man his ghost white hair was combed backward. He was wearing a red dress shirt with a black tie, vest and pants. Dennis couldn't help but feel under dressed as he was wearing his black tie grey pants and jacket then again Mack was wearing his usual red and green Hawaiian shirt with a black T-shirt underneath it and brown khaki pants.

Don Calabresi grinned and removed the cigar from his mouth and placed it in an ash tray on the table. "Benvenuto Mack have a seat" said Don Calabresi, Mack and Dennis sat down in the couch across from him. The picked up a small glass of what Dennis assumed was wine from a table next to his chair and took a sip of it never taking his eyes off of Dennis.

"So what's up boss man?" asked Mack politely.

"Who is this guy?" said Don Calabresi gesturing to Dennis with the glass.

"He's a friend of mine, his name is Dennis" said Mack coolly as he leaned back in the couch.

"Right" said Don Calabresi finally liberating Dennis from his steely eyed glare. Don Calabresi shifted both his gaze and attention to Mack. "I've got a job for you" he said.

"Who's the vic?" asked Mack.

"Last week, an Interpol agent named Mendelssohn shot my brother in a firefight in Paris" said Don Calabresi.

"You have a brother?" Mack replied sounding vaguely surprised.

"Had being the operative term" corrected Don Calabresi.

"Right, so you want me to whack the dude?" asked Mack.

"Yes, such an act must be punished" the Don replied.

As Dennis listened to the conversation he couldn't help but feel like something was up but he decided more out of fear than anything else to keep quiet. Still as they spoke Dennis felt guilty about what he was hearing.

"Mendelssohn won't be in Paris very long so you're going to have to fly over there tonight" said Don Calabresi. "We have an apartment across the street from his apartment, feel free to use it" he continued as he pulled a piece of paper out of his vest pocket and handed it to Mack.

Mack leaned forward took the picture and studied it front and back before placing it in his pocket. "Let's see, you want me to kill an Interpol agent in Paris, this one will cost you around five mill" said Mack calmly.

Dennis watched in in awe at how these two could casually discuss murder like it was a mere business deal. "Very well, I'll pay you through the Guild" said Don Calabresi.

"Bodacious" said Mack, the two men stood up and shook hands.

Dennis sensed it was time to go and stood up only to be followed by Mack and the Don.

"My boys'll take you from here to the airport. You're booked on the first flight to Paris" the Don explained.

"What about my stuff?" asked Mack.

"We've notified the Guild and there's a suitcase with a sniper rifle waiting for you there" said Don Calabresi.

"You've thought of everything" Mack replied.

"I prefer to think of it as the family helping someone who helps it" said Don Calabresi.

"I dig it" replied Mack.

"Good luck" said Don Calabresi.

Mack and Dennis walked out of the room. Standing outside the room was the man they had followed to the meeting. They followed him to the car and drove off to the airport. Once they were gone, there was a knock on the door.

"Come in" said Don Calabresi knowing exactly who it was. The door opened and into the room walked Vito Messana, Don Calabresi's consigliere, looking mildly perturbed as the Don poured himself a glass of wine.

"With all due respect Sir, I have my reservations about this course of action" said Messana.

"You're my consigliere, your job is to second guess me" said Don Calabresi as he took a sip of wine.

"Yes well, Mendelssohn's not even in Paris, so why choose him specifically?" Messana asked respectfully.

"Because Roycewicz knows that we've had some problems with Mendelssohn in the past" replied the Don.

"I see" replied Messana.

"Good, now send the contract to the Guild and make it an open one" ordered Don Calabresi.

"How much should I make the reward?" asked Messana.

Don Calabresi sat quietly for a minute thinking carefully. "Twenty five million, that should bring out the heavy hitters" he answered.

"Right, what about that Dennis guy?" asked Messana.

"He's a loose end so twenty five million for killing both of them" answered Don Calabresi.

"Understood I'll take care of it immediately" said Messana. He hurriedly walked out of the room as Don Calabresi poured himself another drink.

As they drove to the airport they were both quiet. Mack looked over to Dennis with a grin.

"So…ever been to Paris?" asked Mack.

Chapter 14

No Shot in the Dark

After seven hours in the air, Mack and Dennis arrived at Charles De Gaulle airport in Paris. Dennis was glad he had kept his passport in his back pocket so they could make it through customs faster. After what felt like fifteen minutes of going through security they exited the airport. Outside there were several waiting taxis bringing people both to and from the airport. Mack hailed one and told him where to take them in French then handed him a few francs.

"I didn't know you could speak French" said Dennis as the driver pulled away from the airport.

"Yeah, I can speak a few languages actually, it's kind of an unofficial job requirement" answered Mack.

"I can see why" said Dennis.

"It's mostly a few European languages, and some Chinese and Japanese, since most of my work is either here or over there, what about you?" Mack explained.

"I took Spanish in High School, got a C minus" said Dennis as he adjusted his glasses.

"Better than I did in Spanish" grunted Mack.

"I have a question though, since most of your jobs come from Europe, why don't you just move and live here and save money on travel?" asked Dennis.

"Honestly I've thought about it more than once, but I've decided against it" answered Mack.

"Why, is it too expensive for you to live here?" asked Dennis.

"Hell no, I can afford to live here and travel but the reason why I don't want to live here is the terrorism" Mack answered.

"Why terrorism? I would think that would create a lot of potential jobs for you" said Dennis.

"Actually It doesn't, it only makes my job harder" said Mack.

"You see when there's a terrorist attack it's harder to move around in the country because the damn cops are everywhere and everyone's on edge" Mack explained.

"I never thought about that to be honest, but it makes sense" said Dennis.

"Yeah in my line of work terrorism is bad for business" replied Mack.

By the time they arrived at the apartment the sky was pitch black and the city of lights was lit up like a sparkling Christmas tree. The apartment was small with two bedrooms a couch and a kitchenette. Dennis gazed out the window while Mack was in the bedroom retrieving the weapons the mafia had placed there for him. Dennis had never been to Paris let alone outside the United States before meeting Mack.

As Dennis looked out at the sprawling metropolis beyond him it became increasingly difficult to find where the sparkling lights of the city ended and the starry night sky began. Dennis momentarily forgot why his purpose for accompanying Mack to the city as he studied the twinkling Parisian skyline. The buildings were nowhere near as huge as the skyscrapers in New York. In fact the skyline was dominated by the tower of glittering lights in the distance known to the world as the Eiffel tower. The tower was like a column that jutted down from the heavens to touch the world of men.

"Dude, Check it out!" said Mack enthusiastically from behind him interrupting his long distance sightseeing.

Dennis turned around to face him, feeling mildly irritated at being interrupted by him. His piddling irritation was suddenly replaced by curiosity when he saw that Mack holding a large rectangular shaped carrying case.

"I found it" said Mack. Dennis had already figured out was in the case.

The weapons, Don Calabresi said would be waiting here for him. Mack placed the case on its back on the counter in the kitchenette.

"Where was it?" asked Dennis.

"Under the bed" said Mack, as he took off his red and green Hawaiian shirt, revealing a black t-shirt underneath, and opened the case.

He pulled a brown leather cross draw shoulder holster out of the case and slid his arms through it. Then he pulled out his pistol, a Tanfoglio T95 combat. He loaded it and placed it in the holster. Finally he put on his Hawaiian shirt before returning to the suitcase.

"You're not actually going to kill Mendelssohn with that are you?" asked Dennis skeptically.

Mack grinned slyly, "Of course not I'm going to kill him with this bad boy" said Mack.

He reached into the case and pulled out perhaps the smallest, and up till now only, sniper rifle Dennis had ever seen.

"Mr Faraday. Allow me to introduce you to the Russian Vintovka Snayperskaya Spetsialnaya aka the VSS Vintorez" said Mack proudly as he displayed the rifle. "She has an integral silencer and despite looking like the happy meal toy from hell she is very good at cutting through pesky things like body armor" said Mack.

"Okay…So why do you need the pistol then" asked Dennis.

"Two reasons: number one In case shit happens and number two Why not?" said Mack grinning.

Feeling incapable of arguing with such logic, Dennis decided to further the question as Mack returned the rifle to the suitcase and closed it.

"Now let's go ice this dude" said Mack as he picked up the suitcase by its handle with his left hand and walked toward the door. Dennis followed him feeling no recourse. After ten minutes and several flights of stairs they arrived on the roof of the building. He still couldn't get that image of Jimmy The Spaniel being shot out of his head. He squinted his eyes ever so briefly and it was gone. Is this what people like him feel after a kill? He wondered.

The cool night air was refreshing as they were greeted with the sounds and smells of the city. Dennis followed Mack over to the edge of the roof where there was a chimney. Mack crouched down behind the chimney, Dennis crouched down behind him. Gingerly Mack removed the rifle from its case and placed in a fresh magazine and cocked it.

"So where is he?" asked Dennis.

Mack pointed to the building across the street from them to the only window with a balcony on the building. "There" said Mack quietly.

"Let's get this over with" said Dennis as Mack peaked out around the chimney.

Dennis leaned out from behind him as Mack raised the scoped VSS rifle to eye level and aimed it at the balcony. As Dennis watched he noticed movement on the roof of the building with the balcony and a glint of metal. Mack took a deep breath and squeezed the trigger but to his utter shock and disbelief nothing happened. He pulled the trigger again but still no bullets shot forth. Suddenly Dennis grabbed him by the back of his shirt and yanked him back behind the chimney. Before Mack could say anything a machine gun barrage of silenced bullets started hitting the chimney and roof. There was no sound of gunfire just the sound of metal colliding with concrete.

"What the fuck is going on?" barked Dennis trying to keep his head down.

"Hell if I know" said Mack as he tossed the rifle onto the floor and pulled out his pistol.

"What are you doing? Use the damn rifle!" Dennis barked.

"Can't, busted" said Mack drily as he pulled back the slide on the pistol.

"What do you mean it's busted?" asked Dennis.

"I mean it's busted" said Mack as the firing suddenly stopped.

Suddenly Dennis noticed Mack grinning in satisfaction. "What the fuck are you smiling about?" he asked.

"Bastards reloading" answered Mack. Mack quickly leaned out from cover and scanned the roof of the building across the street. He could make out the dark silhouette of something moving on the rooftop. He cursed himself for not having a silencer on his pistol; he aimed his pistol and fired two quick consecutive shots at the black shape praying that he hit the shooter. His prayers were answered when he saw the body of the shooter fall limply off the roof and onto the pavement below. He looked down and saw that the man's body wasn't moving.

"Got him" said Mack nonchalantly, he shifted his attention back to Dennis.

"Who was that guy and why was he trying to kill us?" asked Dennis frantically.

Mack simply shrugged, "I don't know" answered Mack.

"But I'm more concerned with why the damn rifle didn't work" continued Mack.

Mack picked it up and removed the clip and was shocked by what he saw. The clip was full of dummy bullets, which not only explained why the gun didn't work but why the rifle didn't feel lighter in Mack's hand.

"These bullets are fake," said Mack his voice tinged with sudden anger and confusion.

None of them had to say it but they both knew it, it was an inescapable truth: They had been set up, the only question was why.

"So what now?" asked Dennis.

Mack stood there for a minute and returned the rifle and to its case.

"Now we go inside and I'll figure this out" said Mack.

Dennis knowing no other recourse followed him back to the room.

"What about the cops?" asked Dennis once they had returned to the room.

"Not a problem, odds are we'll be long gone before they show up" answered Mack.

Mack tossed the useless crate on the counter and pulled out his cellphone.

"I'm getting to the bottom of this can of shit right now" said Mack as he dialed the phone number of Don Calabresi. He turned away from Dennis as he placed the phone against his ear.

After a few rings he got an answer, "Hello" said Don Calabresi on the other end of the phone.

"Boss! It's MAGIC 44, the bullets in the gun were duds why?" asked Mack.

Don Calabresi sighed, "Because you're a loose end that could trip us up".

"Loose end, what do you mean I'm a loose end?" said Mack incredulously.

"You know exactly what I mean, as of now there is a twenty five million dollar open contract on you and your friends heads" growled Don Calabresi.

"The Guild has revoked your gold status, and before you ask the ammo in your pistol isn't fake, think of it as giving you a sporting chance" continued Don Calabresi.

"Gee thanks, I didn't know you cared" replied Mack sarcastically.

"You know I'm going to kill you for this, right?" growled Mack menacingly.

Don Calabresi laughed mockingly at the threat, "you might as well juggle the Earth and moon".

"If you or your friend so much as set foot in New York or any of our territories you'll be dead before you hit the floor" he continued.

"What about all that "the family helps those who serve it" shit" said Mack.

"The family also protects itself and we are concerned that you have become a liability, besides you two have bigger problems to worry about right now" said Don Calabresi.

Mack knew he was right, a price that high would draw every assassin, Guild member or otherwise, out of the woodwork. Consider this goodbye and also good luck" said Don Calabresi. Before Mack could reply Don Calabresi hung up. Mack returned the phone to his pocket and looked over at Dennis.

"Well?" asked Dennis who was sitting on the couch in the room.

"All right, there's good news and there's bad news" said Mack sheepishly.

Dennis shrugged asking himself how bad the bad news could be. "Ok, what's the bad news" asked Dennis.

Chapter 15

Batman to the Rescue

As Mack calmly explained what the bad news was, Dennis felt like he had just been given a death sentence, each word hitting Dennis with the full force of a sledgehammer.

"Wait, why do they want to kill me? What the hell did I do?" asked Dennis.

"Nothing, it's simply association" quietly explained Mack.

Dennis buried his head in his hands and leaned back into the couch silently cursing himself for going into that bar in the first place and meeting Mack. "I can believe this" he muttered.

"I know right, I worked hard for that gold status," complained Mack.

"What's gold status mean?" asked Dennis.

"Its kind of like a rating system within the Guild" Mack explained. "Gold means you are highly rated blue not so good"

Dennis shrugged, unable to fathom why he was so unfazed by this recent development. "What do we do now? Go to the cops?" asked Dennis.

"Hell no, we do that and the Guild will raise the contract and kill us themselves, besides who the hell would believe any of this shit" said Mack calmly.

"Of course" said Dennis drily as he tried not to think about the price on his head. "Can't you get the Guild to drop the hit or something" he asked.

"Nope, it's all above board a perfectly legal contract" said Mack still as cool as a cucumber.

Dennis's head sank deeper into his hands as he realized how utterly hopeless his situation had become. He almost felt like crying as he slowly began to realize that his entire life had been ripped to pieces. "Dude relax, it's not totally hopeless" said Mack. At this Dennis angrily looked up at Mack and stood up.

"Relax?! How the hell am I supposed to relax? You just told me the mafia placed a hit on our heads" said Dennis furiously.

"We can't go home for God's sake, we are completely and totally one hundred percent fucked!" barked Dennis frustrated.

"I know it sounds like that but really we're only fifty percent fucked" said Mack. "Or maybe eighty percent, I don't know, I suck at math" he continued.

"The fuck does that mean and how can you be so calm about this?" yelled a frustrated Dennis.

"Because of the good news" said Mack.

"What good news? How can there possibly be any good news?" asked Dennis.

"I have a plan" said Mack.

Dennis rolled his eyes as he sat back down.

"Really" said Mack.

"All right what is this all mighty plan?" said Dennis sarcastically.

"There's a place in the Devils Sea called Sankan Island, that's controlled by the Vasilev Syndicate and the Heise She Li Triad" said Mack.

"So?" asked Dennis.

"So, a friend of mine is the head of the Triads operations there. If we go there he can help us" Mack explained.

"And how do you plan to get us there in the first place?" asked Dennis.

"First part is getting out of Europe" said Mack. "Our best bet is to take the train to Batman then hop a flight to Nepal," he continued.

"Wait, Batman?" said Dennis confused.

"Yeah it's a city in Turkey," explained Mack as if that was common knowledge.

"So your telling me that there's a city in Turkey named Batman?" said Dennis with disbelief.

"Yep, fucking awesome right?" said Mack.

"Is there a city called Robin too?" asked Dennis sarcastically.

"Of course not that'd be stupid now if there was city called Nightwing that'd be kickass" said Mack.

"Who the hell is Nightwing?" asked Dennis.

"Robin" answered Mack nonchalantly.

"Right because that makes sense" said Dennis as he rolled his eyes.

"So once we get to "Batman" then what?" asked Dennis.

"Then we get a flight across China to Yokohama and BOOM it's a straight shot to Sankan Island" said Mack.

"All the while avoiding the assassins that will be coming after us right?" said Dennis.

"Exactly, it don't sound that hard" said Mack calmly.

"You came up with this plan in the last five minutes didn't you" said Dennis.

"Pretty much yeah…so you in?" said Mack. Dennis shrugged, realizing he had no other options but to follow Mack to this mysterious island. "Yeah fine" said Dennis still feeling surly.

Suddenly a thought occurred to him as he started pondering his new life on the run. "I'll go but I want a gun" said Dennis strongly.

He immediately felt stupid making the request since he had never fired a gun in his life.

Mack raised his eyebrow in surprise upon hearing the request.

"A gun? Sure I can get you that easy when we get to Batman" said Mack as he pulled out his cellphone.

"What are you doing?" asked Dennis, "calling a friend of mine for tickets" answered Mack nonchalantly.

*****

The basement was dank, dark and cold, in many ways it reminded Sasha Molotova of the interrogation rooms in Red Curtain's underground headquarters. Though with two key differences: she wasn't in Moscow she was in New York and she was no longer an agent of Red Curtain. She had removed her black leather jacket and was dressed in a red tank top, black belt, and black pants. She wiped the sweat from her brow, and sighed out of exhaustion. Sasha picked up one of the water bottles she had brought with her to water board the target and took a long drink.

After conversing with Mack and his friend and getting a drink as well as some information she left the Guilds bar. She tracked down and kidnapped her target: the Aquarius agent known as Karl Stern. She had been interrogating him for hours, though Sasha could tell his resistance was starting to crumble. He sat in front of her naked in a seat less wooden chair with a black bag over his head and several cuts and bruises on his chest and arms, his hands tied behind his back to the chair. Sasha hadn't tortured someone in years but when it came to members of Aquarius she made no exception.

With her free hand she slapped him hard in the face to wake him up.

"Wake up!" barked Sasha.

The man's head rose weakly, "What is Aquarius planning" barked Sasha.

Stern mumbled something in defiance; Sasha couldn't make out what he said either because of the bag over his head or the beating. She shrugged and pulled his head backwards and poured the remaining water on his head. He writhed and moaned in pain.

When the bottle was empty she tossed it on the floor.

"Please stop! I'll talk," gargled Stern.

Sasha pulled the bag off his head roughly.

"What is Aquarius planning?" yelled Sasha loudly.

"I don't know what it is exactly but it's called Project: SPEARHEAD, that's all I know I swear to God" said Stern weakly almost crying.

"Funny, I didn't think Nazis believed in God" said Sasha as she pulled out her pistol, a silenced scoped Mauser c96 broom handle, out of her waist holster.

She cocked it and aimed it at Stern's head, before he could react she pulled the trigger and killed him. The last thing she expected to hear after killing him was the sound of her phone beeping. She pulled it out of her pocket and checked it. She was surprised to see that it was a notification that an open contract had been issued to all Guild members. She was even more surprised to see that it was for Mack Roycewicz and his friend.

She briefly thought about trying to help him but decided against it. After all he can handle himself and I have more important things to deal with right now thought Sasha as she closed the notification and casually returned the phone to her pocket.

*****

"I hate American Chinese food" muttered Deng irritably as he ate take out with Siobhan in the hotel room.

Siobhan looked at him confusedly from across the table.

"That's something you don't hear everyday" said Siobhan sarcastically as she continued eating.

"What?" Deng asked.

"A Chinese man that doesn't like Chinese food, it's unusual" said Siobhan sarcastically.

"I said American Chinese food, they never manage to get it just right here, still least it's not like that haggis crap you people eat" retorted Deng jokingly.

"That's Scottish" corrected Siobhan.

"What?" said Deng.

"Haggis is from Scotland, I'm Irish" corrected Siobhan. "Though I could go for some drisheen since we're on the subject"

"What the hell is drisheen?" asked Deng.

"It's a blood pudding made from sheep's intestines and filled with meal and sheep's blood" answered Siobhan.

"Sounds delicious" said Deng sarcastically.

"Oh it's lovely, personally I like it with breadcrumbs but some eat it with cooked oatmeal" said Siobhan.

"Suddenly this doesn't seem so bad" said Deng looking at his takeout. Just then his phone rang, "excuse me for a minute" said Deng as he pulled it out of his pocket and put it to his ear.

Siobhan could barely understand what the man on the other side of the phone was saying.

"What?!" said Deng surprised and angry. "When?"

"I see. Notify all our operatives to make contact with them immediately if possible, as for us we'll be on our way back" said Deng.

As he hung up and returned the phone to his pocket, there was an irritated look on his face.

"What happened?" said Siobhan.

"That was Mazin, a few hours ago the Scarpetta family put a twenty five million dollar contract out on MAGIC 44" answered Deng.

Siobhan looked at him a puzzled expression on her face. "Why?" she asked.

"Probably just to screw with us, I shuld have known that was why they Calabrsei met with us" said Deng angry at himself.

"Where is he now?" asked Siobhan.

"Apparently MAGIC 44 and some friend of his are in Paris at the moment" explained Deng.

"How is that a problem?" asked Siobhan.

"Because we have barely any presence in Europe" answered Deng.

"Mazin thinks that he's going to try to head to Sankan" continued Deng.

"So where does that leave us?" asked Siobhan.

"On the way back to Sankan" replied Deng bitterly.

"I guess we should pack up then" said Siobhan smugly.

"At least there's better Chinese food there" grunted Deng.

Chapter 16

Escape from the City of Lights

To Dennis's utter bewilderment, Mack had managed to book a room for them on the Orient Express to Turkey. It was still dark outside by the time they arrived at the train station via taxi. The station was surprisingly crowded, despite it being so early, which ironically made Dennis feel claustrophobic. They walked through the train station and got the tickets. It felt surreal knowing that there was now a twenty five million dollar bounty on his life.

Is that all my life is worth twenty five million dollars thought Dennis. As they walked to the train platform Dennis was nervously looking around, expecting an assassin to jump out any minute and kill him.

"Dude, relax no ones' going to try and kill us out in the open like this" said Mack.

"How do you know that?" asked Dennis, "Because it's too public" Mack replied nonchalantly.

"So how exactly did you get us first class tickets on the Orient Express?" Dennis asked, desperate to talk about something else.

"I have a friend in the Union Corse" said Mack.

"The Union what?" asked Dennis, confused having never heard the name before.

"The Union Corse, you know the French mafia?" said Mack.

"There's a French mafia?" asked Dennis wishing he had some coffee before they left.

"Yeah I know crazy right" Mack replied.

"Don't worry, they're great I mean they're vicious killers but they're great" said Mack reassuringly.

"Yeah, because we have such a great history with anything called the mafia" grumbled Dennis sarcastically.

"That's just negative man" said Mack as they boarded the train just as the first rays of morning sunlight began to bathe the city.

As they walked to their room in the passenger car, Dennis noticed that the amount of luggage they had was miniscule compared to what the other passengers were bringing. There room number was 193 and to Dennis's surprise it was more spacious than he expected. There was a small couch in front of the window, a small bathroom, shelves and a bunk bed for them. "What do you think?" asked Mack.

"It's....nicer than I expected" Dennis answered.

"Well yeah, this is the Orient Express not Amtrak" said Mack.

"Now I gotta go make a phone call so I'll be right back" said Mack as he walked out of the room.

Dennis placed his stuff on the bottom bunk and sat on the couch gazing out the window. Suddenly the train lurched forward and slowly began picking up speed reducing the world outside to a formless multicolored blur. Dennis couldn't help but ask himself, is this life now forever on the run. "Well, I've got good news" said Mack as he barged into the room, taking care to close the door behind him.

"What no bad news?" Dennis said sarcastically.

"Not this time, I just got off the phone with a buddy of mine in Batman" said Mack.

"He's arranged passage for us to Nepal and he's got a gun for you" Mack explained.

"Good, how long till we get there?" asked Dennis, "Five days, next stop is Innsbruck then Bucharest and then Voila Batman" answered Mack.

"So what now?" asked Dennis.

Mack simply shrugged. "I don't know; want to get something to eat?"

Now that Mack had brought it up Dennis was feeling hungry. "Yeah, though how can you eat when people are trying to kill us"

"Very easily" replied Mack with his signature nonchalance.

Dennis rolled his eyes and followed Mack to the dining car. The dining car was half-full with people either eating or reading the newspaper. On the right and left of the car up against the windows were red booths with tables in between them. Dennis and Mack sat at a booth across from each other. When the waitress arrived they ordered breakfast and coffee. Dennis ordered whole-wheat toast with bacon and eggs, Mack ordered a Belgian waffle. "So, do you have any idea who might come after us?" asked Dennis.

Mack leaned back in his chair. "Well it's mostly going to be a bunch of goons with guns, although considering the reward is so high, it'll definitely draw out the Guilds top ranked members"

"And they would be?" asked Dennis.

"Sato Masaki for one then there's the Razzle Dazzle twins, maybe BABYLON" Mack explained.

"Who?" Dennis interrupted.

"BABYLON, He's this big crazy Russian guy though we probably won't have to worry about him, since he works primarily in Africa" explained Mack.

Before Dennis could respond a tall arrogant looking man in a dark blue blazer, a white t-shirt with black horizontal lines and black pants, brown jacket, blue shirt and blue pants approached there table. He had a pencil thin black mustache and a black French beret.

"It's been a long time, mon ami" interrupted the man in a heavy French accent.

Dennis and Mack looked up at the man. "Hey DISCUS, how's things" asked Mack drily. Dennis noticed that Mack looked like he had just seen a ghost.

"Bien, allow me to introduce myself Mr. Faraday, my name is Achille Renfroe" said the man as he extended his hand to Dennis. Nervously Dennis shook Achille's hand.

"What are you doing here Achille, last I heard you were in Tadmor prison?" said Mack.

Renfroe sat down next to Dennis ignoring him and focusing on Mack. "I escaped last year, anyway I was taking the train to Budapest for a job when I got the Guild's notice about the contract on you two," said Renfroe.

"I must say Roycewicz, you really screwed up if the Italians want your hide" Renfroe said accusingly.

"We're innocent" said Mack defensively, Renfroe laughed.

"Funny thing about being in prison for two years is that you realize innocence is a lie" said Renfroe menacingly.

"You dropped the soap didn't you?" asked Mack sarcastically.

Renfroe grimaced slightly at the joke though Mack and Dennis could see the hatred in his eyes. "Anyway gentlemen, I came here to tell you this" said Renfroe.

"For the next five days enjoy yourselves because you will both die before you reach Sankan" said Renfroe. "You sure about that?" asked Mack as Renfroe stood up to leave.

"Absolutely, Au Revoir" said Renfroe before walking out of the dining car just as there food arrived.

"We are so screwed" said Dennis.

"Not for the moment" said Mack as he began eating.

"What?" replied Dennis.

"Dude relax, he's not gonna kill us on the train and neither am I because it'd be borderline impossible to hide the body on a train" explained Mack.

Dennis shrugged and tried to put Renfroe's prophecy out of his mind. "So, who was he exactly?" asked Dennis.

"French assassin his codename is: DISCUS, his specialty is throwing razor sharp Frisbees at his target" said Mack in between forkfuls of Belgian Waffle.

"He kills people with razor edged frisbees?" said Dennis thinking Mack was joking.

"Seriously, razor-edged Frisbees," said Mack confirming it.

"Hell of a way to die" muttered Dennis.

"I know right, I mean exploding baseballs would be way better" replied Mack nonchalantly.

Dennis decided to change the subject. "I was thinking about what you said in Paris over the phone"

"Yeah, what about it?" asked Mack as he reached for his coffee cup.

"Well it doesn't make sense, you said we're going to Sankan yet you told Calabresi that you were going to kill him as revenge" answered Dennis as Mack took a sip of coffee.

"Oh…that yeah, I just said that to scare him" answered Mack as he returned his cup to the table.

"So you're not going to kill him?" said Dennis surprised.

"Pretty much" said Mack casually.

"Why? After what he did to us how could you not want to kill him?" retorted Dennis, his voice tinged just a little with anger.

"Oh no don't get me wrong, I'm pissed off at the bastard but the way I see it revenge is just too gnarly man, not to mention bad for business" said Mack.

"Gnarly?" asked Dennis confused at his meaning.

"Yeah you know gnarly" Mack replied.

"I get how it would be bad for business but how is revenge gnarly?" asked Dennis.

"Dude, over the years I have witnessed first-hand what revenge does to people, it consumes you until there's nothing left of you but an angry husk" explained Mack.

"And I don't need that shit in my life" Mack continued.

Dennis was silent for a minute as he thought about what Mack said.

"Good point" said Dennis.

"Tell me about it" replied Mack dismissively.

"By the way you going to eat that?" asked Mack gesturing to Dennis's toast with his fork.

Chapter 17

Middle of the Road

It was the late afternoon when the Orient Express arrived at the train station in Batman. By the time Mack and Dennis had gotten through customs it was almost evening. The terminal was packed with people shuffling about. Dennis followed Mack outside of the terminal, his nervousness about Achilles threat had faded and been replaced by curiosity about Mack's contact in the city. While Mack hailed a taxi, Dennis looked around for Achille but didn't see him.

After a few minutes a yellow taxi pulled up and they got in carrying the little luggage they had with them. "Take us to this address" said Mack as he handed the man a piece of paper with some money. The driver nodded and pulled away from the station.

"So what now?" asked Dennis.

"We go see my contact Demir and he'll take us out of the country and get you that gun you wanted" replied Mack.

Dennis had almost forgotten about the gun but remembered it when Mack mentioned it. "Who is this guy anyway?" he asked.

"He's an arms dealer with a plane that'll get us to Nepal" Mack answered.

Dennis rolled his eyes sarcastically, "So we're putting our lives in the hands of an arms dealer?" asked Dennis skeptically.

"Pretty much yeah" replied Mack bluntly.

"Why are we putting our lives in the hands of an arms dealer" asked Dennis.

"Well aside from owing me a few favors, he's really good at getting in and out of countries without alerting anyone" Mack answered.

"Right" replied Dennis still feeling skeptical about the tactic.

"By the way have you ever fired a gun?" Mack asked curiously.

"No" answered Dennis, embarrassed at the answer.

"Huh, don't worry about it I'll show you," said Mack nonchalantly. "Everything goes according to plan you'll never need it" he continued.

"And if they don't go according to plan?" asked Dennis.

"Then do what I do and improvise" said Mack with a grin.

Before Mack could formulate a response the taxi stopped in front of a four story building in a rundown segment of town.

"Good, we're here" said Mack, as they got out of the car with their stuff.

Mack waved to the driver who nodded and left. Dennis followed Mack into the building, through the empty lobby and up a seemingly endless flight of stairs. "So who is this Demir guy exactly?" Dennis asked.

"Well he's former Turkish air force then he used to be a pilot for Windwaker Transports now he's working solo" answered Mack.

"As an arms dealer?" Dennis asked concernedly.

"Hey man, it's a job" answered Mack dismissively just as they reached the top of the stairs. In front of them was a large metal door with the number four written on it in both Turkish and English. Mack opened the door and walked into a hallway with Dennis following him.

On both sides of the hall were wooden doors that Dennis assumed were offices for different people. They stopped at a door that had the words: Emperor Eagle Services written on the window in Turkish and English. Mack removed his black tea shade sunglasses and opened the door and they walked inside. They were standing in a room with a dark green carpet and two chairs against the left wall. On the opposite side of the room was a raisin-faced woman of about sixty sitting behind a desk, cluttered with papers and smoking a cigarette while working on a computer seemingly oblivious of Mack and Dennis's arrival.

Before Mack could say anything the woman pointed to the door behind her with a bony wrinkly finger and said "He's waiting for you" in a voice that sounded like rocks being crushed.

"Thanks" said Mack as he and Dennis walked to the door, the woman grunted in annoyance.

They entered a medium sized office with bookcases on the left and right walls. In the middle of the room was a cluttered wooden desk with a computer and a phone on it. Seated behind the desk speaking onto a cellphone in Arabic was an older man with white streaks in his hair and a black goatee wearing a dark grey jacket and blue jeans. In front of the pile of clutter was a brass sign with the words Demir Adem CEO written in both English and Turkish. He motioned to Dennis and Mack to sit in the two chairs in front of the desk.

They sat down and waited for him to finish talking on the phone. After a few seconds he hung up the phone and shifted his attention to Mack and Dennis. "Hey Demir, how's things?" Mack asked.

"As well as can be expected" replied Demir.

"So same old same old then?" asked Mack sarcastically.

Demir laughed, "how are you my friend it's been too long" said Demir warmly. "Could be better, still having a problem with Cobalt?" Mack asked.

"Of course my friend, now what can I help you with?" answered Demir.

"Like I said over the phone we need a lift to Nepal asap" said Mack.

"May I ask why?" Demir inquired.

"Let's just say the shit hit the fan and it got everywhere" Mack answered.

Demir chuckled at the analogy, "and you can't clean it up?" asked Demir.

"Yeah, it got everywhere" replied Mack.

"It just so happens that I was about to leave anyway" said Demir. "You see I'm going to be flying a shipment of Ak-74's to a Tibetan freedom group in western Tibet tonight, If you'd be willing to help with security I can give you both a lift to Kathmandu" he explained.

Mack thought hard for a minute, "Alright you've got a deal" said Mack. The two men reached across the desk and shook hands in agreement.

"Oh, before I forget, Mr. Faraday I managed to procure this for you" said Demir as he opened a drawer on his desk and pulled out a metal lockbox. He handed the box to

Dennis; gingerly Dennis took the box knowing full well what was in it. He opened it and picked up what was inside taking care not to aim it at anyone.

"That is a Sig Sauer P230 chambered for a .32 ACP round and modified for a suppressor" said Demir.

Dennis looked into the box and saw a brown single draw shoulder holster, two magazines and a black tube which Dennis assumed was the suppressor. "Thank you, how much is it?" asked Dennis as he returned the gun to the box and closed it.

Demir raised his hand in protest, "Consider it on the house"

"By the way Mack, I'm curious why come to me for this and not Cobalt?" asked Demir shifting his attention to Mack.

"Because Neubauer is nuts" Mack answered.

"Agreed, now let's get going the plane should be done fueling by the time we get to the airfield" continued Demir.

Demir stood up and walked out of the office with Dennis and Mack following behind him.

As they walked down the stairs Dennis leaned over to Mack. "Who's Neubauer and what's Cobalt?" whispered Dennis.

"My biggest rival in the arms trade" answered Demir bluntly. Dennis was off put by the suddenness of the answer.

"And Neubauer is what the CEO or something?" asked Dennis.

"Bingo" answered Mack as they arrived at the bottom of the stairs. They followed Demir through the lobby to a parking garage across the street. As they approached Demir's car Mack suddenly grabbed both of them by the backs of their jackets and threw them to the ground before jumping onto his stomach.

"Stay down!" yelled Mack as he instinctively, reached under his red Hawaiian shirt and into his holster for his pistol only to remember that he had left it in the suitcase.

Before either of them could speak a knife flew overhead and embedded itself into a cement pillar next to Demir's car. Mack recognized the knife and knew instantly who it belonged to. "Dennis! Slide me the box!" whispered Mack. Dennis instantly realizing what Mack's intentions were slid the box over to him.

"I can't tell you how long I've waited for this moment" yelled a familiar voice from the dimly lit part of the parking garage in front of them.

"Get behind the car" whispered Mack as he opened the box and removed the P230 and a magazine.

He crouched and ran over to the back of the car with the others. "Mack I'm not going to get killed today so kill that son of a bitch" grunted Demir.

"Good Idea" said Mack as he slid the magazine into the butt of the P230. He pulled the slide back stood up and aimed it but quickly ducked as another knife flew overhead almost slicing his head clean off. Before he could do anything, a barrage of machine gun bullets sprayed the other side of the car.

"Come on, give me a challenge!" yelled the familiar voice this time sounding more cocky. Seeing his opportunity Mack jumped up with his gun in hand.

"I got your challenge right here asshole" yelled Mack as he aimed the pistol in the direction of the gunfire and fired three shots just as another knife came flying at him missing his head by mere inches and hitting the car.

"Damn" muttered Mack as he glanced at the knife surprised at how close it had come to hitting him.

Mack quickly ran over to where the shots and knives had come from. Mack saw Sato Masaki laying on the floor, still alive but bleeding from his stomach and shoulder. Sato desperately reached for the machine pistol lying next to him. Mack kicked the gun away from him. "Sorry Sato, but you know what they say don't bring a knife to a gun fight" said Mack as he aimed his pistol at Satos head.

"Damn you" coughed Sato.

"You wish" replied Mack before pulling the trigger and killing him.

Mack knelt down and picked up the MPL submachine gun beside him and walked back to Dennis and Demir.

"Who was it, DISCUS?" asked Dennis.

"No, Sato" Mack replied.

"We should get going the police will be here soon" said Demir.

"Lead the way" said Mack as he and Dennis picked up there stuff and placed it in the trunk of his car.

"By the way Dennis I believe this is yours" said Mack as he handed the pistol butt first to Dennis.

"Thanks" said Dennis as he took the pistol and returned it to the box. Demir got in the driver's seat and started the car and Dennis and Mack got in the back seat. Mack put on his sunglasses as Demir backed out of the parking garage and drove away.

*****

Two hours later they arrived at an airfield outside of the city. The only structure was a dilapidated hangar in front of it was a dark gray C-27J Spartan cargo plane outside of it. They pulled up to the hanger and got out. "Gentlemen I give you the Aluminum Falcon!" said Demir proudly gesturing to the plane.

Mack removed his sunglasses, "It's supposed to be the Millenium Falcon Demir" said Mack.

"Aluminum Falcon sounds better" protested Demir confidently.

"No it doesn't" argued Mack, Dennis stepped forward.

"As long as I'm the pilot it does" Demir grunted.

"Your plane your rules" said Mack with a shrug.

"That's some plane is it yours?" said Dennis curious as to the planes model and wishing to change the subject.

"Yes it is. It's a C-27J Spartan used to belong to the Americans now it's mine" said Demir proudly.

"How'd you get it?" Dennis asked.

Demir grinned, "A gift from your countries intelligence agency" said Demir slyly.

"The CIA?" said Mack his voice tinged with a hint of concern.

"Who do you think hired me to get these guns and give them to the Tibetans?" said Demir.

"Look Demir, I don't want to get mixed up in some CIA shit show I've already got plenty of assholes trying to kill me" Mack said.

"Relax, they don't know you're here besides everything's going to go according to plan" said Demir. "Now excuse me I have to go prep the plane" he continued before boarding the plane.

"Mack, a word" said Dennis gesturing to him that he wished to talk in private.

"What is it?" asked Mack as if he knew what Dennis was going to ask.

"Are you sure we can trust this guy?" asked Dennis quietly.

"Probably, he's never steered me wrong before" replied Mack with a shrug.

"How sure" asked Dennis.

"I don't know, like seventy percent" answered Mack with a wave of his hand.

"Seriously?" replied Dennis annoyed and feeling nervous.

"Hey could be worse" said Mack.

"How?" answered Dennis.

"Could be ten percent, now c'mon lets go" said Mack before walking over to the planes side door.

Dennis shrugged and followed him into the plane just as the propellers began to spin.

Chapter 18

Claws of the Emperor Eagle

The airplane shook waking Dennis from his sleep, he was lying on his side on the benches against the side of the plane. He had draped himself in a blanket to shield himself from the cold. In the middle of the plane were two crates that Demir said were filled with the weapons and ammunition they were going to be delivering to the Tibetans. On a swivel next to the side entrance was an M60 machine gun with a tarp on it. He still couldn't believe that this was his life now; traveling with an assassin to an island he had never heard of to avoid the hit men trying to kill them both.

He sat up and looked around the dimly lit interior of the plane in search of Mack. Suddenly the cockpit door swung open and Mack walked out. His was wearing his brown khakis and black tea shade sunglasses' and his red and green Hawaiian shirt was buttoned. There was a look of mild surprise on his face. "Ah dude, your awake" said Mack as he removed the glasses from his face and placed them in his shirts chest pocket.

"Yeah where are we?" asked Dennis as he rubbed the sleep from his eyes.

"Well we entered Tibetan airspace an hour ago so we should be landing soon" said Mack as he sat down next to Dennis.

"So who are these guys we're taking these guns too exactly?" asked Dennis.

"Demir told me all about them, they're called the Tibetan Resistance Armada they've had some skirmishes with PLA forces in the area" Mack explained.

"What's the PLA" interrupted Dennis.

"Chinese army" replied Mack dismissively.

"So why didn't you just say that" asked Dennis sarcastically.

"I wanted to be accurate" said Mack dismissively.

"Right, so what do they want anyway?" Dennis inquired feeling somewhat stupid for asking the question.

"To get China out of Tibet or some shit like that" replied Mack disinterestedly.

"You sound like you don't approve" said Dennis.

"Thing is I've seen people like them all over the world man they're all the same, a bunch of suicidal kids blinded by ideology and politics" said Mack.

"Once you've seen the shit I've seen you figure out that politics and ideology is just code for bullshit" said Mack.

"That's...quite a philosophy" replied Dennis.

"Hey man, call it what you will the fact is life is a hell of a thing" Mack said.

Casually Mack pulled out his pistol out of his shoulder holster.

"What are you doing?" asked Dennis watching curiously.

"Checking my gun" replied Mack.

"By the way, where's yours?" asked Mack as he casually removed the slide of the Sauer in his hand to check it for any irregularities.

"Under the seat" said Dennis as he proceeded to pull the box out from under the seat.

"Good, I was afraid that you lost it or something" replied Mack as he put the slide back on the gun and returned it to his left holster and picked up the other one and began to check it.

Dennis opened the box and removed the pistol so he could study it more in depth. While he had never fired a gun before, he had enough common sense to keep his finger off the trigger, especially since he was on an airplane. He briefly wondered if he could use it if he was forced to. He glanced back at Mack who was still checking his pistol when something occurred to him. "I have a question, why is your gun bigger than mine?" he asked.

"Because, I'm better with guns than you" said Mack,

"That's fair…I think" Dennis replied.

"Don't worry if you practice you can go all John Woo on peoples asses" said Mack.

"John Woo?" asked Dennis confusedly.

"Yeah, you know a pistol in each hand? Doves flying everywhere?" explained Mack as if it was common knowledge.

"Why? It seems like that wouldn't be very accurate, plus I only have the one gun" pointed out Dennis.

"It all depends on how good your aim is" answered Mack as he finished checking the pistol.

"And it looks cool right?" Dennis replied.

"Now you're getting it" answered Mack slyly as he pulled a magazine out of his pocket and slid it into the butt of the gun.

"Then how come you don't use two?" asked Dennis.

"Because I'm good but I'm not that good" answered Mack.

Suddenly Demir's voice blared over the intercom, "prepare for landing" said Demir.

"Time to make the magic happen" Mack said as he cocked the pistol and slid it into his holster.

"Wait, where are we landing?" asked Dennis nervously.

"An abandoned airstrip in the mountains" said Mack nonchalantly.

"One thing though, let Demir do all the talking" continued Mack his voice suddenly dead serious.

Dennis nodded and removed the shoulder holster from the box and slid it on. As Dennis pulled out the gun and placed it in the holster Mack watched studiously.

"One more thing, unless the shit hits the fan keep your hands away from that gun at all times, these people will take any excuse to shoot you" said Mack as he gestured to the ground.

"And if the shit does hit the fan?" Dennis asked.

"Then shoot the fan and duck" replied Mack dismissively.

"Anywhere in particular" asked Dennis still getting used to the reality that he might have to kill someone.

"Chest, but if you get an opportunity aim for the head" answered Mack.

"Got it" replied Dennis, he had been watching Mack handle his pistol. The plane glided to the runway, shaking upon contact with the ground. Dennis instinctively closed his eyes as they skidded down the runway assuming the worst was about to happen. To his relief the plane slowly stopped like it was supposed to. Mack and Dennis stood up, Dennis took a breath of relief until he realized that the worst was yet to come. Demir exited the cockpit and casually walked past them to the other side of the plane.

Demir pulled a lever on the wall and the rear cargo door of the plane and with a loud mechanical hum the cargo door slowly moved backward onto the ground. Dennis surmised that they would slide the crates down the door like a ramp. The cool night air wafted into the plane as Mack and Dennis followed Demir out of the plane via the ramp. The sky was a pitch black, ebony blanket interrupted only by the twinkling stars the moon and the distant snowcapped mountains. The dilapidated airstrip was flanked by forest. In the distance Dennis could see the Himalayas. Surrounding the airstrip was a rusty chain mail fence. Dennis shivered a little since he was not used to the chilly mountain air.

Slowly approaching them was an old military looking truck. "Ah, they're here" said Demir approvingly as the vehicle parked next to the plane.

Once the truck had stopped eight armed, desperate looking, hardened men dressed in green camo disembarked from the truck. Dennis noticed that all of them were wearing an orange sash or bandanna. Two men stepped out of the front of the truck. Two of the men walked up to Demir, Mack and Dennis while the others kept an eye on them. One of the two men was wearing a necklace with words in Tibetan written on it and was carrying a briefcase handcuffed to his wrist.

The other man was wearing a camo jacket and red beret, on his jacket was a tag that said Choden in Tibetan, Dennis assumed he was the leader and the man with the briefcase was his assistant.

"Mr. Adem, Do you have my equipment?" said Choden in perfect English.

"Depends, do you have my money?" replied Demir.

Choden sighed and pulled a key out of his pocket, handed it to the man with the briefcase. The other man un-cuffed the briefcase and handed it to Demir. "It's all there in cash" said Choden.

"I'm sure it is, still nothing leaves this plane until the money is counted" Demi replied sternly. He handed the briefcase to Dennis, "Dennis count it" said Demir forcefully.

"What?" said Dennis stunned "you heard me, there's supposed to be five million in there, count it" Demir replied. Not knowing what else to do, Dennis nodded and took the briefcase.

Dennis walked into the plane and placed the suitcase on one of the crates then opened it. Upon seeing the briefcases contents Dennis's mouth went dry. Inside was five million dollars in unmarked U.S. dollars. Never in his life did he think he would be this close to five million dollars. Dennis started counting trying not to think about the consequences of being wrong. After ten minutes of counting and counting again he wiped the sweat from his brow and closed the briefcase, silently praying he hadn't miscounted the money. He walked back to Demir, Mack and the two men. "Well?" said Demir.

"It's all there, all five million of it" said Dennis nervously.

Demir grinned in satisfaction, "well then, I guess our business has been concluded gentlemen the guns are yours" said Demir. Choden stepped aside and motioned for his men to enter and take the guns. Suddenly there was a loud crack and Choden's head exploded into bloody fragments of bone and brain.

"Holy fuck!" Dennis yelled at the sudden death.

A second crack and the same fate befell Choden's assistant. Before anyone could react, two large trucks with the logo of the People's Liberation Army of China emblazoned on its side crashed through the chain link fence. Out of the trucks ran ten armed Chinese soldiers screaming at the Tibetans to surrender. The

Tibetans replied by shooting at the soldiers. "Fuck me!" barked Mack angrily as he pulled out his pistol.

"Dennis lets go" barked Mack as he quickly pulled back the pistols slide to cock it.

Dennis ran into the plane narrowly avoiding getting shot in the chaos. Mack fired several shots at the soldiers while backing up into the plane. Demir ran into the plane, stopping only to grab the suitcase, he entered the cockpit and started the engines. Dennis sat inside feeling useless as Mack ran inside the plane. Mack pulled the lever and the cargo door began to close. "What do we do, who are they?" yelled Dennis as he sat down next to the M60.

"Well Sundance, that's the Chinese army and we're getting the fuck out of dodge" Mack barked.

"Mack get on the M60 now!" Demir yelled from the cockpit. Mack smiled like a kid on Christmas morning at the order.

"I always wanted to fire an M60" said Mack as he holstered his pistol.

"What's an M60?" yelled Dennis as Mack ran over to the gun.

"Dennis, this is an M60" said Mack as he pulled the tarp off the gun revealing it to Dennis. It was belt fed and mounted on a monopod that swiveled into the window. Mack opened the window and loaded a belt into the chamber from the ammo box beneath it. Mack pulled back the hammer and looked up at his targets. As they were rolling down the runway, the PLA soldiers having either killed or arrested the Tibetans had devoted their full attention to the fleeing plane and had begun firing at it.

Mack fired in short bursts strafing the area with bullets killing some soldiers and wounding others. Dennis watched him shift from target to target feeling even more useless. One of the trucks drove up alongside them, the soldiers inside trying to hit them with a barrage of automatic fire. Mack aimed the M60 at the truck and fired at it.

Suddenly the plane began to tilt slightly and rise into the air. The sudden tilt caused Dennis to lose his balance and fall backward. He fell down the hull of the plane and was stopped by hitting one of the crates with his head. As the plane got higher and higher in the air Mack continued firing at the truck until it exploded beneath them. The explosion shook the plane but it continued to climb. "Yahoo motherfuckers!" yelled Mack triumphantly as the truck blew up beneath them.

"Dennis you see that?" said Mack as he closed the window and turned to face Dennis.

"Dude you look like you were in a slasher movie" said Mack as he saw him.

"What?" asked Dennis confused.

"Here" said Mack as he handed him a mirror.

Dennis looked in it and was horrified, his shirt, glasses and face were covered in blood. "Oh my God!" said Dennis terrified.

"Dude relax at least it's not yours" said Mack.

"Not helping" snapped Dennis as he frantically tried to get the blood off himself.

"Hey Demir!" yelled Mack.

"What?" replied Demir from the cockpit.

"Got an extra shirt, Dennis got messy" replied Mack.

"Yeah in the closet in the back" replied Demir.

Mack got up and walked to the closet, Dennis was too busy removing blood from his glasses and face to notice. Mack returned with a clean, white, short-sleeved dress shirt. "Dude, you look like a used tampon, take this" said Mack as he held up the shirt.

"Thanks" said Dennis realizing his shirt was too far-gone. He took the blood-drenched shirt and tie off and put the new one on followed by the tie. Feeling slightly better he looked next to him and saw Mack sitting next to him.

"Seriously   though   a   used   tampon?" Dennis said.

"What? I thought it was funny" said Mack. Overwhelmed by everything Dennis fell to the floor unconscious.

Chapter 19

Out of the Blue

Mazin ran as fast as he could to Deng's office with the email he had received from the Triad's man in the PLA. Deng sat in his office, annoyed at his failure to find MAGIC 44 in New York. He sat at his desk, gazing out the window overlooking Sankan and ruminating about another way to find MAGIC 44. Ever since he and Siobhan returned to Sankan, two days ago, he had been trying to conceive of some way to locate MAGIC 44. Yet so far he had failed to think of a solution.

Suddenly there was an excited knocking on the door, interrupting his contemplations. Deng swung his swivel chair around to face the door. "Come in" barked Deng with a sigh and a good idea of who it was. The door swung open and into the office ran Mazin clutching a piece of paper with a large pleased grin on his face.

"Well, Mazin you look like you're having a nice day" said Deng sarcastically.

Before Mazin could speak he bent over and placed his hands on his knees, breathing heavily. "Give me a minute please, Sir" said Mazin as he tried to catch his breath.

"You look like you need two" said Deng smugly leaning back in his chair.

Admittedly he was curious, as he had rarely seen Mazin this excited before. After a few seconds Mazin stood up straight, straightened his tie and sat down in a chair in front of Mazin's desk. "Sir, we found him" said Mazin bluntly.

"What, MAGIC 44?" Deng replied Deng.

"Yes, surprisingly" said Mazin.

"How?" Deng asked.

Mazin leaned forward and handed Deng the paper he had been clutching. "I notified all our global branches to be on the lookout for him, ironically it wasn't one of them that found him"

"I know and?" asked Deng impatiently.

"One of our guys in the PLA did" said Mazin. "Yesterday the PLA raided a compound of Tibetan Freedom Fighters while they were buying guns from a Turkish arms dealer"

"And guess who the arms dealers security was?" continued Mazin.

"MAGIC 44" said Deng grinning at the development.

"We're not entirely a hundred percent sure but it's a strong possibility" answered Mazin.

"He's an assassin that wears a Hawaiian shirt, how can you not be sure?" asked Deng sarcastically.

"Well a lot of people wear Hawaiian shirts Sir" replied Mazin drily.

Deng glared at him unamused with his humor before returning his gaze to the paper before noticing something odd. "It says here that there was someone else with them" said Deng looking up from the paper.

"Oh…that, no one knows who he is" said Mazin feeling a little embarrassed.

"So what happened? does the PLA have them?" asked Deng, shuddering at the thought because if the PLA had them then they were as good as dead.

"That's the best part, they managed to take off and are heading to Nepal as we speak" Mazin said.

"How do you know they're going to Nepal?" asked Deng.

"My PLA contact managed to get me the planes heading once I heard that I instructed our people to start looking for it and they found it via satellite" answered Mazin.

"Who's the arms dealer?" asked Deng.

"Demir Adem, of Emperor Eagle services" answered Mazin.

Deng thought for a for a few seconds. Suddenly he snapped his fingers in sudden realization, "I think I know what he's doing"

"Which is?" asked Mazin.

"He's coming here" answered Deng.

"I don't understand" replied Mazin.

"Think about it, not only does his route hint at it, but the Mafia has put a multi-million dollar bounty on his head thus bringing every Guild assassin out of the woodwork looking for them" said Deng. "Realistically Sankan Island is the safest place for him"

"With all due respect Sir, the last thing Sankan could be called is safe" said Mazin.

"True, but he's probably going to ask either us or the Russians for asylum" answered Deng.

"I see. So, now what?" Mazin asked.

"Make sure he comes to us and not the Russians" Deng replied.

"Obviously but how?" asked Mazin.

"Well they're most likely to head for Yokohama next, so we send someone to meet them when they get there" said Deng.

"Who do you have in mind?" asked Mazin.

Deng thought for a few minutes carefully, "Hire Flying Fish to take Siobhan to Yokohama, pick him up and bring him back" replied Deng. "Why?" asked Mazin.

"Because I want a representative of ours to contact him and Flying Fish is good at getting in and out of places with no one noticing" Deng answered.

"With all due respect, that Cuban woman might complicate things" said Mazin.

"Be that as it may, they do get the job done regardless" replied Deng.

"Right then, I'll call them immediately" said Mazin.

"Good, but seeing as how this is incredibly important, I think you should personally go down there with Siobhan and hire them" said Deng as Mazin stood up to leave.

"Understood Sir," replied Mazin before turning to go to the door. As he closed the door behind him Mazin exhaled nervously before heading to Siobhan's room.

***

The Flying Fish trading companies building was located in Sankan Cities Harbor. It had two floors and served as the living quarters for the companies three employees: Fiona Ramos, Kenji Yamada and there boss Ben Martin. Parked outside in the water was the company's primary delivery vehicle: a modified Grumman HU-16 albatross seaplane affectionately referred to as the Rumrunner. They often served as the delivery company for the Triad, the Vasilev Syndicate and the other criminals that inhabited the Island. They were all former members of the United States Marine Corps Force Recon with a tattoo on there right arms.

They were a Motley Crue however each of them had their own uses and roles. The team's leader, muscle and brain was Ben Martin. He was a tall imposing, muscular, bald African American man dressed in a green camo jacket with a short sleeve black t-shirt underneath it and black pants with a belt holster for his Desert Eagle. Fiona Ramos was a muscular yet attractive Cuban American woman that served as the team's enforcer and weapons specialist. She had light brown skin and was dressed in a short-sleeved white crop top, blue jean short shorts and black leather fingerless gloves.

The hair on the right side of her head was shaved off and her short black hair was brushed to the left side, around her neck were a pair of goggles. Kenji Yamada was a Japanese American with spiky black hair and a goatee. He was dressed in a dark red T-shirt and black and gray camo pants with a belt holster. He served as their sniper and resident mechanic. At the moment Kenji was working on the plane's engine outside while Martin was in his office doing some paperwork and Fiona was reclining in a chair her feet resting on a table sleeping with her head phones on listening to music.

Suddenly Ben heard the gravelly sound of a car pulling up. Ben heard it first, and shifted his gaze to Fiona. He was pleased to see that she had her shoulder holster on containing her two Smith and Wesson 645 pistols, nicknamed Bart and Lisa. "Yo, Fiona! Wake up!" barked Martin loudly as he kicked her chair.

"What!" growled Fiona irritable and short tempered as usual.

"We got company" said Martin.

"Dammit" grunted Fiona as she got out of the chair.

"This better be fucking good" groused Fiona as she removed her headphones and followed Martin over to the window.

"Who the hell is it?" Fiona inquired.

"Looks like the Triad, still only one way to find out" answered Martin. They walked outside with Fiona just as the car pulled up. As he walked outside Martin reached into his jacket pocket and pulled out his reflective aviator sunglasses and put them on. Kenji had already climbed off of the plane and walked over to join them. Parked in front of them was a black sedan with black tinted windows. Out of the car stepped Mazin dressed in the black and white suit of the triad.

"What's with the Ozzy shades?" asked Fiona mockingly. Mazin removed his glasses ignoring Fiona's flippant remark and shifted his attention to Ben.

"Mr. Martin, we have a job for you and your team" said Mazin.

"Must be pretty important if Deng sent you all the way over here to tell us that" Kenji observed.

Mazin laughed, "Actually I'm only here to offer you the job and deliver the package to you should you accept" said Mazin.

"Package?" asked Martin raising his eyebrow in curiosity. In response Mazin opened the door of the car and out stepped Siobhan. She was dressed in her black and white nun's habit with her golden cross necklace around her neck. Before any of them could reply Fiona broke out laughing hysterically.

"You can't be fucking serious?" laughed Fiona. "The package is a Goddamn nun" continued Fiona unable to stop laughing.

"Well…that's new" said Kenji drily.

"I assure you, appearances can be considerably deceiving" Mazin said cryptically.

Over the years the Flying Fish trading company had transported all sorts of illicit cargo for the Triad but they had never transported a nun before. "What's the job? She a hostage or something?" asked Martin.

"I am forbidden to give you the exact details, but you are to take her to Yokohama where she will pick up…an associate and then you will fly her and the associate back to Sankan" Mazin explained.

"Uh huh and this associate would be?" asked Martin.

"An old friend of ours" replied Mazin vaguely.

"Standard Taxi mission then, so let's see Yokohama and back that'll be around 50,000 American" replied Martin.

Mazin bit his lip annoyed at their price, "Fine, You'll be paid upon your return, when can you leave?" answered Mazin.

"That depends, Kenji how's the Rumrunner?" said Martin shifting his gaze to Kenji.

"Fine, I just finished changing the oil so she's good to go whenever you're ready" Kenji answered.

"Excellent. We need you to leave immediately, is that a problem?" asked Mazin.

"Not at all" said Martin.

"What? Come on boss why do have to haul this Jesus freak all the way there?" barked Fiona annoyed.

"What else are you going to do Fiona, sleep?" said Martin.

"Beats listening to Mother Teresa over there singing about heaven and hell all the way to Japan" said Fiona pointing to Siobhan.

"I don't sing" said Siobhan drily.

Fiona shrugged and walked away complaining in Spanish under her breath. Martin extended his hand to Mazin and the two men shook hands, cementing the deal. "Kenji, Fiona get your stuff, I'll get the plane ready" said Martin as he turned to walk toward the plane. He suddenly realized that he had forgotten something. He turned around to face Siobhan.

"By the way, what's your name?" asked Martin.

"Siobhan Costello" answered Siobhan drily.

"What the hell kinda name is that?" asked Fiona.

"It's Irish am I right?" asked Martin, Siobhan nodded signaling yes.

"Great, not only is she a Jesus freak she's also a fucking Leprechaun" grunted Fiona.

Chapter 20

Around and Around

The images that flashed before Dennis were of his average childhood in Baltimore. Every event and moment in his life was flashing before him: his birthdays, learning to ride a bike, to drive school. It was like watching a movie on the screen of his memory. Suddenly he felt a hard slap across his face painfully bringing him back to reality. It took him a few seconds to remember where he was. Standing over him was Mack, "Dude you okay man?" said Mack sounding concerned.

Weakly Dennis sat up and looked around to try and get his bearings, he was laying on top of the wooden crates that they were going to give to the Tibetans. Dennis sat up and rubbed his head, to his surprise there was a bandage wrapped around his head. Instinctively He reached for it. "Don't, you fainted so we had to bandage you up" said Mack.

"What happened? Where are we?" Dennis asked.

"Whoa, whoa, slow your roll man one question at a time" said Mack as he backed away and held up his hands.

"Now to answer your questions: Everything went to shit in Tibet but we got out of there okay and now we're about to land in Tribhuvan airport in Nepal" Mack explained.

"Then what?" asked Dennis as he rubbed his bandaged forehead.

"Then it's only a ten hour flight to Haneda International and finally a three hour boat ride to Sankan" Mack answered.

"Why take a boat to Sankan?" asked Dennis.

"Number one: the airfield there can't accommodate a commercial airliner. Number two: no airline or pilot would go to Sankan, place is a damn cesspool" explained Mack.

"So why are we going there?" Dennis asked confused.

"Because I have friends there" said Mack as he sat down in a chair and strapped in.

Dennis could tell what was about to happen and quickly scampered off the crate, got in a chair and buckled in. Once he had strapped himself in Mack snapped his fingers. "Oh, I forgot" said Mack as he pulled out Macks glasses out of his shirt pocket.

"You dropped these" said Mack casually as he handed the glasses to Dennis.

Dennis sighed and put the glasses on, the plane landed smoothly and they taxied to an inactive runway. A few minutes after landing the Mack and Dennis removed their guns and placed them in their suitcases then disembarked via the side door of the plane. "Thanks for your help, Demir" said Mack as the two men shook hands.

"Me too" said Dennis as he shook the man's hand.

"Think nothing of it my friends" replied Demir as he turned to board his plane. "I have to go, good luck my friends" he continued right before he closed the door.

"I'm getting tired of asking this but what now?" said Dennis as he began to taxi away for takeoff.

"Now you follow me" replied Mack. The two of them snuck into the airport and got some tickets for the first available flight. After going through airport security and surrendering there baggage to the gaping maw of the conveyor belt, they boarded a Japan Airlines 747 and waited for takeoff. Dennis leaned back in the soft comfortable chair, a far cry from the hard plastic seats he and Mack had been traveling in for the last few days. Eventually the plane began to barrel down the runway rising higher and higher into the sky. Next to him sat Mack who was busy reading the dinner menu.

After several hours into the flight, the flight attendants began to take orders from the passengers. When one of them approached Mack and Dennis she found them reclined in their seats fast asleep. The flight attendant, a young attractive Japanese woman, poked them gently and asked what they wanted to eat for dinner. Dennis half asleep glanced at the menu and ordered chicken salad while Mack ordered braised pork on steamed rice. When the waitress returned with their food Dennis ate a few bites and then fell asleep while the waitress stayed to talk to Mack giggling occasionally.

*****

At that moment, above the cerulean waters of the Devils Sea flew the Rumrunner en route to Yokohama. There were three rows of seats in the plane each with three seats, in the back was storage space for cargo. The front row was for the pilot and copilot, the second and third row were for passengers. In total the plane could carry as much as ten people including the pilot and copilot. In the pilot's seat was Ben Martin next to him acting as his copilot was Kenji Yamada. Behind them sat Fiona chewing gum bored, in the back row reading a bible sat Siobhan.

Tired of chewing gum, Fiona reached into her pocket and pulled out her Mp3 player. She put on the headphones and scrolled through the songs eventually settling on one. She selected Same old Situation by Motley Crue then raised the volume as high as it would go finally she clipped it to her shirt and hit play. Eventually she began nodding her head to the music as if at a concert. Siobhan tried to ignore the music but after the first minute of loud music which was easily audible despite the headphones she closed her bible.

Politely Siobhan tapped on Fiona's shoulder, angry at being interrupted Fiona stopped the music, removed the headphones and turned around to face Siobhan.

"What?!" barked Fiona.

"I'm sorry to bother you miss, but your music is too loud would you mind lowering the volume please?" Siobhan asked politely.

In front Ben and Kenji who had been listening grinned. "This is gonna be good" muttered Kenji.

Fiona looked at Siobhan with a face of livid rage. "Bitch! Did you just tell me to turn off Motley Crue?" said Fiona seriously.

"Yes, is that a problem?" Siobhan asked politely.

Fiona was somewhat blindsided by Siobhan's polite response. "I ain't turnin off shit, now go back to your coloring book" replied Fiona brusquely as she put the headphones back on and resumed listening to the music.

Siobhan, still annoyed by the music and by Fiona's lack of cooperation, shrugged her shoulders with regret. "Forgive me my lord" whispered Siobhan as she looked up. Her eyes zeroed in on Fiona's neck and with one sharp calculated blow to Fiona's neck knocked her out. She looked up and saw the faces of Ben and Kenji looking back out her.

"She will awaken in a few hours feeling fine" said Siobhan calmly before returning to her bible.

"Good to hear" said Martin. "We're about to land, after that we use the outboard motor in the pontoons to ride into the harbor"

The plane landed outside the harbor with no problems, after fifteen minutes of maneuvering through the crowded seaways of the port of Yokohama, via the concealed outboard motors in the Rumrunners pontoons, they parked next to one of the docks. The three of them exited the plane and stood on the docks.

"Need any help?" asked Kenji.

"No thank you" replied Siobhan as she began to walk away.

"I have to say you are easily one of the more pleasant people we've transported" said Ben.

Siobhan smiled warmly. "Thank you"

"One more thing" said Ben as she turned to leave.

He approached her menacingly and moved his face close to hers. "I don't care if you are who I think you are, Fiona may have been a pain in the ass but if you lay a hand on one of my crew again not even God can save you from me" said Martin grittily.

Siobhan stared back at him impassively and unthreatened. "You'd be surprised what his grace can save you from" she said unimpressed before walking away.

*****

After sleeping for several hours, Dennis awoke from his sleep. In front of him was the dinner he ordered earlier. To his surprise Mack was gone, everyone else was asleep. He was about to consider waking somebody to ask them where Mack was. Suddenly Mack came walking down the aisle, seemingly out of nowhere, and sat down next to him. Curiously there was a smile on his face evocative of complete satisfaction and pleasure. "What are you so happy about?" Dennis asked.

"Ever been to the Mile High Club?" replied Mack.

"What are you…" said Dennis just as it dawned on him what the Mile High Club was.

"Dude seriously" said Dennis at a loss for words.

"Yeah, man Mile High Club" replied Mack proudly.

"With, who?" asked Dennis afraid to hear the answer.

Mack leaned into the aisle and pointed to the flight attendant who brought them there food.

"Why?" Dennis asked.

"Dude, what's your problem man what are you a sex-ed teacher or something?" replied Mack.

"Aren't we supposed to be incognito or something?" said Dennis defensively.

"Dude, I told you no one's going to try to kill us on an airplane" replied Mack.

"Now excuse me I need a nap, making sweet love in an airplane is tiring" said Mack as he leaned back in the chair and went to sleep.

"I'll bet" replied Dennis wishing he could have come up with something better to say.

Chapter 21

Death at Roads End

As they exited the plane at Haneda International Airport in Tokyo, the flight attendant winked at Mack with a grin. He smiled back at her as Dennis just rolled his eyes exasperated by the whole affair. After going through airport security they walked to baggage claim and collected their luggage. Then they walked to the Keikyu station and boarded a train to Yokohama station. Dennis was glad that they wouldn't be flying anymore as he was already starting to feel jet lagged.

Dennis looked out the window of the train at the sunset in the distance. It was a beautiful sight, the waning sunlight reflecting off the skyscrapers as the sun slowly disappeared behind the snow-capped grandeur of Mount Fuji. Dennis looked over at Mack who was checking his phone. "What are you doing?"

"Looking for a boat to charter to Sankan" Mack answered.

"Hey, there's something I was wondering about" said Dennis.

"Shoot" replied Mack looking up from the phone.

"You know where I'm from because of my book but I don't know where you're from" answered Dennis.

"Seaside Heights, New Jersey" replied Mack.

"Huh, when I was younger my family used to vacation up there in the summer" said

Dennis surprised at the answer although it did explain Mack's accent.

"No way, small world right" said Mack, "yeah definitely" said Dennis. He was mildly surprised at how soon they arrived at Yokohama Station. He checked his watch out of curiosity. "Huh, eleven minutes"

"Yeah, gotta love Japanese engineering man" replied Mack as they joined the mass of people exiting the train. As they walked through the train station Mack's phone started beeping. He pulled it out of his pocket to check it and as he studied the screen.

"Bitchin" muttered Mack grinning with satisfaction as he looked at the message on his phone.

"What is it?" Dennis asked.

"Good news, I just got a notification that there's a fishing boat willing to take us to Sankan" answered Mack.

"Good, how much is it going to cost and come to think of it how have you been financing this odyssey to begin with?" Dennis asked.

"Dude, I have made a lot of money doing this job" answered Mack.

Dennis decided not to press the issue further. Upon exiting the train station Mack hailed a taxi. After a few minutes a taxi pulled up and they placed their suitcases in the trunk and got in the back of the taxi. "Take us to pier nine Yokohama Harbor" said Mack in Japanese as he handed the man a wad of cash.

The driver nodded, shifted the car out of neutral and pulled away from the train station. After about an hour of driving through the neon illuminated streets of Yokohama night had fallen on the city. The car slowed down as they drove through the harbor until they reached pier nine. The pier consisted of rows of silver warehouses next to the water. The driver parked in front of two of the warehouses.

Mack and Dennis exited the taxi, retrieved their luggage and waved farewell to the driver. He nodded back at them and drove off. Once he was gone they looked around studying their surroundings. The pier was empty and dark. The only light came from lights on the sides of warehouses. Behind them were two warehouses with a small alleyway between them that was ominously shrouded in darkness. In front of the warehouses was the pier. "Looks like a great place for a murder" said Mack sarcastically.

"Yeah that's reassuring" Dennis replied drily.

"So, where's the boat?" asked Dennis as he looked at the pier.

"What are you talking about?" said Mack confused as he turned to look at the pier.

"The boats right over" said Mack stopping as he saw that there were no boats at the pier at all.

"Where the hell's the boat?" exclaimed Mack.

"You haven't realized it yet?" said a familiar sounding voice in a heavy French accent from the alleyway behind them. Instantly Mack and Dennis turned around to discover the owner of the voice.

"Oh shit" muttered Mack. Suddenly out of the shadowy alleyway flew a small disc shaped object. Mack and Dennis jumped out of the way narrowly avoiding getting hit. Slowly a man walked out of the alleyway. Mack and Dennis looked up at him as he stepped into the light. He was dressed in a dark blue blazer and black pants with a white t-shirt with black stripes on it. In his left hand glistening in the moonlight was a razor tipped Frisbee.

"Achille" Mack growled.

"At least you managed to figure that out MAGIC" said Achille Renfroe with an arrogant smile.

"Do you idiots have any idea how easy it was to track you here" said Achille smiling.

"Do you have any idea how little we care?" Mack grunted sarcastically.

"Believe me you will" replied Achille with a creepy smile.

"I must say, I'm glad you managed to survive that idiot Masaki because now I get the satisfaction of revenge" continued Achille as he reached into his blazer to pull out another frisbee.

Before he could finish Dennis lunged at him with all of his strength knocking Achille on the ground. Renfroe looked at Dennis with a look of pure hatred and within seconds was on his feet. Achille ran at Dennis, Dennis pulled back his arm preparing to throw a punch. Renfroe caught the punch in his hand and Dennis in the stomach with his left knee. "Little man, wait your turn" said Renfroe angrily as Dennis writhed in pain on the ground.

Achille smiled sadistically as he shifted his attention to Dennis's hand. Renfroe squeezed his hand until there was a barely audible crack resulting in an anguished yelp of pain from Dennis. Before Masaki could break another bone Mack kicked him in the back of the leg causing Achille to release Dennis. Mack grabbed him by the back of his jacket and threw him to the ground. "You broke his hand, wanna break mine?" said Mack as he walked over to Achille.

"Absolutely" said Achille smiling creepily as he jumped to his feet.

"Dennis you okay?" asked Mack glancing over at Dennis.

"Please kick his ass" Dennis groaned as he clutched his hand.

"He won't" said Achille as he reached for another Frisbee.

Before he could throw it Mack struck him in the face with his left hand. Mack threw another punch at him, Achille shrugged off the blow and almost sliced off Mack's head with the Frisbees edge but he ducked. Mack jumped up hitting Achille in the face with an uppercut. Achille staggered backward, then with lightning speed lunged at Mack hitting him with multiple lightning fast blows to

Mack's chest and face. As Mack desperately tried to block the punches Dennis, ignoring the throbbing pain in his hand, crawled over to his suitcase knowing the key to victory lay inside.

With a particularly hard punch Achille knocked Mack to the ground, his face covered in cuts and blood. Weakly, Mack stood up, his fists raised in defense, Achille grinned slyly.

"Are you simply too stubborn to admit that your beaten?" said Achille.

Mack grinned, "What does beaten mean?"

"Stop!" barked Dennis, They looked over at Dennis and saw him aiming his pistol in his other hand.

"Dennis, shoot the bastard" said Mack.

"He won't, he's not like us Roycewicz he doesn't have the balls" said Achille arrogantly.

"You sure about that?" said Dennis as he pulled back the hammer cocking the pistol.

"Your hand is shaking, you can't do it so just lay down and die" said Achille as he slowly approached Dennis. Instinctively Dennis kept on backing away from him, his hand shaking.

"We're not done here" said Mack as he grabbed Achilles shoulder.

Achille spun around and backhanded Mack with his fist knocking him to the ground. "We most certainly are" said Achille smugly as he turned to face Dennis. As Dennis was backing away he bumped into the warehouse and knew he could back away no more.

"End of the line" gloated Renfroe.

Dennis closed his eyes and tightened his grip on the gun. Suddenly a shot rang out, echoing across the harbor. Dennis opened his eyes and saw Achille standing in front of him blood pouring out of his shoulder, his face in utter shock. Mack, with his remaining ergs of energy jumped up and grabbed Achille from behind and threw him into the water. Exhausted, Mack fell to the ground weakly, Dennis fell to the ground smiling and feeling exhausted. His body, slumped against the building Dennis heard footsteps approaching from the left. Weakly he looked in the direction of the footsteps but couldn't tell who it was. It appeared to be a woman dressed in black and white.

Suddenly it occurred to him that he didn't feel his arm snap back following the gunshot. He tossed the gun to the side too weak to care. "Mack you okay?" yelled Dennis weakly, after a few seconds.

"Not particularly" grunted Mack as he lifted his head up to look at Dennis. His nose and mouth were bloody and bruised from the fight.

"Well, we've got company" groaned Dennis as he started to lose consciousness as the footsteps got louder and closer.

"Great, say hi for me" said Mack as he closed his eyes as he lost consciousness. "Tell her yourself" moaned Dennis before falling to the floor unconscious.

Siobhan approached them, glanced at the two unconscious bodies on the ground and holstered her Colt .45. She pulled out her cellphone, dialed a number and waited for answer. "Yes?" Ben replied.

"I need you and Mr. Yamada over at Pier nine immediately I found them" said Siobhan.

"Gotcha, we're on our way" said Ben before ending the call.

As Siobhan returned the phone to her pocket, she wondered whether to bring both of them or just Mack.

"Lady I don't know who the hell you are but whatever you want me for he comes with me" groaned Mack momentarily lapsing back in consciousness.

Siobhan walked over to him and looked him straight in his eyes. She could tell that he meant it. If they were to accomplish their task for Deng then it would be placate the man.

"So be it" said Siobhan.

"Good" muttered Mack as his eyes closed once again fading away.

She walked away from their unconscious bodies and began collecting there things. Just as she had finished returning Dennis's gun and glasses to its suitcase, she noticed a pair of black tea shade sunglasses on the ground. She picked them up dusted them off and placed them in her pocket.

Chapter 22

Sunrise over Hell

It almost felt like a dream, Dennis awoke in a clean bed in what appeared to be a hotel room. Outside he heard the typical sounds of a city, for a minute he wondered if he was back in New York and if the last few weeks were but a dream. Weakly he got out of bed, as he stood up he noticed that not only was the pain from the fight gone but he was dressed in a hospital gown and his broken right hand was in a white plaster cast. He walked over to the window and opened the blinds bathing him and the room in sunlight. The city before him was like nothing he had ever seen.

He could tell he was on the upper floors of a tall skyscraper due to the view. The skyline of the city was dominated by one other skyscraper across the street. Every other structure in the city appeared to have only three or four floors. In the distance, Dennis saw what appeared to be a small mountain range dominated by a large mountain on the horizon. The surrounding city appeared to be, even from a distance, incredibly poor and dilapidated.

"How the hell did I get here?" muttered Dennis as he tried to remember how but the last thing he remembered was saying something to Mack.

Dennis shifted his attention to the room, wishing to put on some clothes. Across from the bed was a wardrobe, he opened it and saw his gray pants, white dress shirt and black tie cleaned and folded on the bottom of the wardrobe. On the table next to his bed were his glasses, which he could tell had been cleaned, and his wallet. Quickly Dennis got dressed and put on his glasses, ignoring the bursts of pain from his broken hand. After getting dressed he looked around for his phone and gun but he couldn't find either one. Suddenly there was a loud knocking on the door. Mack shrugged, approached the door and opened it.

Dennis was both surprised and relieved to see that on the other side of the door with a grin that reeked of success, dressed in his buttoned red and green Hawaiian shirt and light brown khaki pants, stood Mack Roycewicz.

"Well Dennis, we made it bro" said Mack proudly. He wasn't unscathed either, there were several cuts on his face and some bandages on his arm.

"What do you mean we made it? Where are we and how are we not dead?" Dennis asked.

Mack held up his hand, "Whoa slow down kemo sabe, we're about to find out from the man himself" said Mack reassuringly. "By the way how's the hand?" asked Mack.

In response Dennis held up his hand with the cast on it. "Hurts like hell but I'll manage"

"Good, because the man wants to see us now" replied Mack.

"Who exactly is "the man?" Dennis asked.

"Follow me" said Mack as he turned to leave, Dennis shrugged and followed Mack. Dennis followed Mack down a hallway lined with rooms on both sides to the elevator at the end of the hallway. They got inside and rode to the top floor. "So how badly did you get hurt?" asked Dennis as the elevator continued to climb.

"Just a few cuts and a broken rib" said Mack drily.

Before Dennis could reply the elevator stopped and the doors opened. They stepped out onto the roof. Dennis was at a loss for words by what he saw. The roof of the building was a small garden with a stone walkway that led to a cul-de-sac with a

Chinese man and a woman seated at a table drinking tea. They walked out of the elevator.

"You think this is crazy, look behind you" said Mack gesturing behind him as they walked to the table.

Dennis turned around and saw a giant red pagoda with two floors, a balcony and a helicopter on the roof. "This is incredible"

"I know right" Mack replied.

As they approached the table the man and woman stood up to greet them. The man had short black hair. He was wearing a white dress shirt, black tie with black pants and a black trench coat. But what made no sense to Dennis was the woman next to him, out of the four of them she was easily the tallest. She had pale skin, a voluptuous body, and red hair with a golden cross necklace around her neck. What was the most confusing thing about her though was that she was dressed in the clothing of a catholic nun.

"Welcome to Sankan Island gentlemen, my name is Deng" said the man politely.

"This is my associate Sister Siobhan Costello" he continued as he gestured to the nun, she nodded at them in response.

"Please have a seat" said Deng politely.

Mack and Dennis sat at the table as Deng returned to his seat and the woman sat down.

Chapter 23

Devil's Garden

Mack studied Siobhan for a minute trying to figure out why she looked familiar. "Wait, this might sound crazy but she looks a hell of a lot like".

"The Devil Woman?" interrupted Deng.

"She is or rather she was, now she works for us" he explained.

At hearing this Mack leaned back in the chair his eyes locked on Siobhan.

"That can't be Mack told me she's dead" said Dennis skeptically.

"I faked it" Siobhan replied bluntly.

"Hey man if anyone could have faked death it would be the Devil Woman" said Mack.

"That's another thing, stop calling me that, I am no longer the Devil Woman I am a servant of the lord" said Siobhan forcefully with a glare that could melt steel.

"The Lord? Is that what you've got her calling you Deng?" Mack asked with a sarcastic grin.

"No, I prefer the name Angel of Vengeance now" answered Siobhan.

"That's badass" grunted Mack.

"I think we've lost the plot here people" said Deng with a grin. "I bet your wondering how and why you're still alive"

"You could say that" said Dennis, Deng shifted his attention to Dennis.

"I have questions of my own Mr. Faraday, however since your my guests you ask your questions first" said Deng as he leaned back in his chair.

Dennis and Mack looked at each other confused as they tried to figure out who would speak first. "I guess I'll go first" said Mack as both men returned their gaze to Deng.

"Let's start with the obvious one: How are we still alive?" Mack inquired.

"Ah, a simple question with a not so simple answer, you see we have been tracking you for some time Mr. Roycewicz. We almost had you in New York but we lost you, then we managed to locate you in Tibet," said Deng taking a short pause for effect.

"Once we realized you were coming here I dispatched Ms. Costello to go to Japan, intercept you and bring you back here" continued Deng pointing to Siobhan with his thumb. "However, by the time she located you two, you were both getting the hell beaten from you by that fool Renfroe, and so Siobhan had to save you"

"We brought you both back here and put you both back together" Deng finished.

"So we got saved by a nun?" said Mack.

"Yes" grunted Siobhan.

"Excuse me, but I think the bigger question is, why track us in the first place?" Dennis asked.

"And what do you want from us that would make you go to such extremes?" asked Mack. "And finally how the hell did you get the Devil Woman to work for you?"

Deng smiled, "Good questions all, but you are in error Mr. Faraday you are inconsequential it is only Roycewicz that we need," said Deng.

"Whatever it is you want us for Deng he comes with" said Mack defiantly.

"Ah, I see my apologies I did not realize that this was a package deal, we are amenable to that" replied Deng.

"Now what do you want us for?" asked Mack.

"Before we get to that I have a question of my own, Mack, I've known you for a long time, so I have to ask why the hell are you being followed around by this man?" said Deng pointing to Dennis.

Mack and Dennis looked at each other trying to figure out how best to explain it.

"Here's the short and simple version, He was following me around doing research for a book about and then the shit hit the fan and he's basically following me around now as a friend and confidant" said Mack.

"That's not very short or simple" said Deng grinning sarcastically.

"You don't know the half of it" Dennis interjected.

Deng laughed at Dennis's witticism, "No I don't, but it sounds interesting" said Deng.

"Now what are we here for anyway?" asked Mack.

"Gentlemen, to truly answer that question I have to give you a bit of a history lesson" said Deng.

"There's no homework is there?" asked Mack sarcastically.

Deng smiled at the wisecrack, "For decades we of the triad have been the undisputed overlord of crime in Asia, our only major rival is the Vasilev Syndicate from Russia" said Deng pointing to the tower across the street from them.

"However for the past twenty years we have been at war with an enemy as invisible as it is powerful, they want control of both our territories and the Russians" said Deng.

"They are so powerful and omnipresent they even managed to kill the Mountain Master's wife years ago" continued Deng.

"The Mountain Master?" asked Dennis.

"The head of the triad" said Mack quietly.

"What are they called?" Dennis asked.

"That's actually one of the things we do know about them, they're called the Networc" answered Deng.

"Never heard of them" interrupted Mack.

"No one has heard of them it's like they're a ghost, well everyone except one" answered Deng.

"Who?" asked Dennis.

"A former CIA agent named Simon Kane, five months ago we discovered that the Networc killed his wife and we contacted him with an offer" continued Deng. "If he protected the Mountain Master's daughter we would help him find and destroy our mutual enemy"

"And how do you intend to do that?" asked Dennis, "By assembling a team to assist him, we've already got one member" said Deng gesturing to Siobhan.

"And now we have another...with an extra" said Deng pointing to Mack and Dennis.

Mack whistled impressed with the plan. "Wasn't expecting that shit"

"So, gentlemen the question is simple are you in or out?" asked Deng.

Chapter 24

Three Down — None to Go

"What if we say no?" Mack asked.

"That is not a good idea, just know that you will be under our protection as long as you are working for us meaning no Guild assassin will touch you plus the money would be too much to say no" said Deng. "And you know what happens to those who incur our wrath"

"Can we talk this over?" Dennis asked .

"Of course" said Deng as he stood up left the table with Siobhan following him. They walked over to the pagoda where Deng and Siobhan could not hear them.

"You think they'll go for it?" asked Siobhan.

"They'd be fools not to" replied Deng.

"What do you think about them?" asked Deng.

"The offer is too good to decline without due consideration" replied Siobhan.

"True, but that's not what I asked you" said Deng. "I asked you, what do you think about them?"

"Honestly, Mack seems capable but lacks discipline and Dennis has never fired a gun and can't fight making him a liability, and with their injuries" said Siobhan.

"They can heal and he can learn, do you think you can work with them?" interrupted Deng.

"If I have to, but it will take time for them to heal" answered Siobhan.

"Time you can spend developing a rapport with them" Deng grunted.

At the table Dennis and Mack sat quietly waiting to see who would speak first. "Well, I'll say it I'm in, what about you?" asked Mack.

"Is there really no other option?" asked Dennis.

"Dude! It's us, a ninja nun and a CIA agent going up against the fucking Illuminati what's not to love?" replied Mack with a grin on his face.

"We don't know these people though" protested Dennis.

"I do and besides what could go wrong?" argued Mack.

"That's what you said about Paris and Tibet" Dennis complained.

"Look, sometimes you got to grab life by the horns and ride it to the end" said Mack.

Dennis thought about it for a minute, this whole adventure with Mack was built on that concept and he had to admit he was intrigued by this Networc. But he knew that it went deeper than that, not only was it too late to back out now but Mack was his friend and he wanted to see this to the end. "You know what fuck it, I'm in" said Dennis as the two men shook hands.

Mack grinned like a kid on Christmas at the answer, "Bodacious"

Mack turned and waved to Siobhan and Deng to come back to the table.

Mack and Dennis returned to Deng and Siobhans table walked over and sat down.

"So, gentlemen what's the word?" asked Deng.

"We're in" said Mack.

"Excellent" said Deng.

"However, we can't do anything until we get these casts off" said Dennis as he raised the cast up to show them.

"Of course, we will do everything we can to accelerate your convalescence" said Deng.

"Sweet, by the way when do we meet this Simon Kane joker?" asked Mack.

"At the moment, he's in Tangier acting protecting the daughter while she's doing charity work" answered Deng.

"When you're both recovered, which should be in two or three weeks, I'll summon them back here and we can get down to business" responded Deng.

"So what do we do in the meantime?" asked Dennis.

"You can get rest here and train yourselves" replied Deng glaring at Dennis.

The four of them stood up and shook hands cementing the deal. "Now then, follow me, we have lunch prepared in the living room" said Deng.

"Great, I can't remember the last time I ate" Mack grunted.

*****

Dennis and Mack returned to their hotel rooms well fed and tired. The food was exquisite and the conversation fascinating. Tomorrow, Mack would show Dennis how to shoot and handle the gun. Dennis locked the door to his room, deSiring only sleep. He walked over to the window to gaze out at the city once more.

The sun was just beginning to set on the cursed city of Sankan. Dennis felt almost guilty for eating well when the impoverished people below had to beg for food. His thoughts changed to anticipation to tomorrow and the days beyond. He almost felt like he had been reborn as he thought about the events of the last few weeks. He closed the blinds of the window turning the room dark except for the small beads of light that eked through the blinds.

He placed his glasses on the nightstand next to his bed and lay down and slowly began to drift off into sleep. After lunch, Deng had retired to his office feeling proud of himself for having assembled the team before the Mountain Master's deal with Kane expired. He sat in his chair and loosened his tie feeling like the master of the universe as he gazed out at Sankan below him. He closed his eyes and started humming the song "Another one bites the dust" by Queen. His revelry was interrupted by the ringing of his cellphone.

Annoyed he removed it from his pocket and saw that it was from the Mountain Master, Lin Yunao, he answered the phone.

"Yes Sir" said Deng.

"Is everything ready" asked Lin.

"Yes, when Simon and Mai return we will be ready for Phase two" said Deng.

"Excellent" replied Lin over the phone.

Thank you for reading Death Dealers Incorporated. Please remember post a review on Amazon.com

Simon Kane returns in
Book five of the
Shadow World Saga

No One Lives Forever....